# 新版多益測驗攻略
# New TOEIC
# Test-Preparation Guide 2

## 200 TOEIC Test Questions

高 志 豪
羽角俊之  著

○

Recorded by

Thomas J. Brink

Terri Pebsworth

Scott Barber

Riana Rose-Neva Young

GLOBALmate Co., LTD.
全球模考股份有限公司

## Acknowledgments

The following individuals provided invaluable assistance in the development of this book:
Christopher Heintz, Thomas J. Brink, Terri Pebsworth, Scott Barber, Riana Rose-Neva Young

ETS, the ETS logo, and TOEIC are registered trademarks of Educational Testing Service.
This publication is not endorsed or approved by ETS.

 http://www.toeic.com.tw

 http://www.toeicok.com.tw

 http://www.englishok.com.tw

 http://www.globalmate.com.tw

http://online.globalmate.com.tw

# 全球模考股份有限公司
# TOEIC叢書簡介

- 本書「**新版多益測驗攻略**」New TOEIC Test-Preparation Guide 2 係*TOEICmate Series*叢書第二冊，原為2008年「新版多益測驗指南」初版、再版之第二組試題，本版次為改版，即修訂再版。

- *TOEICmate Series*叢書共四本，書名如下：

  > 1、新版多益測驗指南(2010年6月改版一刷)　　CD為New TOEIC試題題解本1
  > 2、新版多益測驗攻略(2010年6月改版一刷)　　CD為New TOEIC試題題解本2
  > 3、新版多益測驗解析(2010年4月再版一刷)
  > 4、新版多益測驗導引(2010年4月再版一刷)

*TOEICmate Series*每書均包括一組200題完整長度的仿真*TOEIC*測驗題組，和CD一片及聽力原文。此外，更附加由**高志豪**老師所撰寫的文章--或單字記憶、閱讀方法，或聽力技巧、文法要點，或常考單字、片語、文法規則…等引領讀者英語學習的方法，可供讀者參考。

- *Manhattan Series*叢書共二本，書名如下：

  > 1、新多益精選集(2010年7月初版)
  > 2、新多益實戰集(2010年8月初版)

*Manhattan Series*每書均附一組*Sample Test*和完整的200題*TOEIC*仿真測驗，並加上解答、單字表，以及中文翻譯。另有CD一片和聽力原文。

## 作 者

**羽角俊之** | Hasumi Toshiyuki

| | |
|---|---|
| ・2005年~現在 | 從事TOEIC教學五年餘,教學單位有補習班、公務機關、民營公司和大學院校等,大約二十餘個單位。 |
| ・2007年~現在 | 撰寫TOEIC、TOEIC Bridge相關書籍四本及多種講義教材。<br>獲得以下認證:<br>・中華民國國際職能教育發展協會TOEIC、TOEIC Bridge 師資培訓合格證書<br>・TOEIC 990 滿分(1次傳統、9次新版多益滿分)<br>・全民英檢高級通過 |

**高志豪** | Simon C.H. Kao

| | |
|---|---|
| ・經　　歷 | 【聯合報】副刊「智慧的火花」專欄之特約英文翻譯<br>亞洲作家會議期間,擔任【中央、中華日報】特約韓文翻譯<br>【中國時報】人間副刊先讀為快專欄「星星的故鄉」之特約韓文翻譯 |
| ・2006年7~9月 | 主持編譯ETS官方版傳統多益全真試題3組,迷你全真試題2組(2006年9月底由忠欣公司出版兩本書)。 |
| ・2007年5~7月 | 主持編譯ETS官方版新版多益全真試題2組 (2007年7月中旬由忠欣公司出版 **New TOEIC** Official Test-Preparation Guide 一書)。 |
| ・2006年3月~<br>　2007年12月 | 主持編譯TOEICmate系列傳統仿真試題,共11組完整試題 (全球模考出版TOEIC叢書九本)。 |
| ・1995年~2010年 | 從事TOEIC課程教學16年,教學單位有協會、基金會、公務機關、民營公司和大學院校等,大約近百個單位。撰寫**TOEIC**相關叢書五本以及講義教材不計其數。 |
| ・2001年~2010年 | 從事TOEIC相關的演講9年,演講單位有協會、基金會、補習班、公務機關、民營公司、大學院校、國中、高中等,演講超過200場次。 |
| ・2004年~2010年 | 從事TOEIC**師資培訓**教學6年餘,培訓單位有補習班、協會、大學院校、國中、高中等,培訓英語師資超過2,200位。 |
| ・2006年~2010年 | 擔任全球模考股份有限公司負責人,主持TOEIC、TOEIC Bridge叢書和其他英語叢書的出版工作。 |

# CONTENTs

# 字彙篇

### 發揮聯想和意會的創意能力

## 活背單字樂趣多 首部曲

**背英文單字常因愈背愈多，記到後面，忘了前面。如此一來，學習英語的信心全無，變成一件苦差事！怎樣活背單字，充份運用想像力，享受事半功倍的樂趣？**

「英文單字的記憶」，是所有英語學習者「心中永遠的痛」，筆者以為這種說法並不為過。

在英語學習的過程中，筆者和所有人一樣，常為單字的記憶而煩惱，也常為單字的貧乏不足，而望文生畏、望書興嘆！因此，一度發願背單字，渴望能記住上萬個生字，期待有朝一日，看英文書報，就像看中文書報一般。

筆者在高一時，背單字的方法，是效法愚公移山的精神，買了一本小字典，打算「**一個蘿蔔一個坑**」地逐字背完整本字典。於是懷著理想：每天背一頁，每天撕去一頁，就像撕掉牆上的日曆一般。結果理想變成了幻想，而幻想則破滅了。因為，小字典只撕了三、四頁，就再也撕不下去。原因是：記到後面，忘了前面，老是丟三忘四。如此一來，學習英語的信心全無，背英文單字則成了一件苦差事！筆者到了高二，「背生字」的技巧和方法，卻有了重大的轉變和突破。因此，使得單字能力遽升到兩萬多字，其過程幾可用「**茅塞頓開，豁然貫通**」來形容。

從此，筆者對學習英文的興趣大增。這些年來，更因為工作的需要，英文成了筆者不可或缺的工具。回憶起這段學習英語的歷程，個中酸甜苦辣，現在回味起來，則又「**別是一般滋味在心頭**」！

如今，藉著本書《新版多益測驗攻略》，發表「**活背單字樂趣多**」系列短文，旨在將筆者學英語的一愚之得，野人獻曝一番。希望對讀者們在單字的記憶方面有所助益，進而提高學習英語的興趣和信心！且讓筆者學那「白頭宮女說前朝」，一一娓娓道來——

### ● 充分運用聯想和意會的能力

人的右腦掌管「圖像、色彩、音樂、方向」的作用，其創造聯想、意會的潛能

無限，人們卻極少開發、利用它。如果能多加運用個人的想像力、創造力，就可以很快記住任何事物。但是，這得全憑個人的體會和領悟了。就記憶英文單字來說，確實需要一些聯想和意會的創意能力。例如——

easy chair，照字面上看來，是「輕鬆的椅子」。仔細聯想一下，那麼豈不是「安樂椅」嗎？

easy payment 輕鬆的付款，意會一下，自然就是「分期付款」的意思了。

至於 passive smoking 被動的吸煙，就是所謂的「吸二手煙」。吸二手煙的人應是在吸煙者 smoker 旁邊，被迫吸進煙吧！

fatheaded 是「肥的腦袋的」，豈不是和 pigheaded「豬的腦袋的」一樣？一定是「愚鈍的、愚頑的」意思！

再想想看 conundrum 這個字，拆開來是 co-（英文字首，定義為 with，together）和 nun（尼姑、修女），以及 drum（打鼓）。於是 conundrum 可以記成「尼姑一起打鼓」，這好像是出一道「謎」一樣，所以 conundrum 是「謎」的意思，這不就記住囉！

再看看 pop-top 這個字，pop 是「啵」的聲音，top 是頂端、上面。如果你要打開易開罐飲料，就必須將罐頂的拉環拉掉。一拉拉環，罐子上頭就發出「啵」的一聲，所以「易開罐」就是 pop-top。因為要拉開拉環，所以也叫作 ring-pull。

ghostwrite，本來是人寫東西，卻找了鬼來寫；ghostwrite 豈非「代人捉刀、代筆」的意思？ ghostwriter 自然是「槍手、捉刀者、代筆者」了。

late night snack 晚的晚上的點心，可知是「宵夜」；coffee-table book 咖啡桌（茶几）的書，一定是「消遣性的書籍」，鐵定不是國統綱領或三民主義啦！

● **矛盾的造字**

當然，有時造字者心不在焉，或我輩悟性太差，怎麼想也想不通單字的本意，而這單字本身確實構造矛盾，例如：sweetmeat（甜點、蜜餞）是 sweet 甜的，固然不錯，可是並非 meat（肉）。倒是 sweetstuff 比較名符其實；stuff 是「物品」，甜

的物品 sweetstuff，當然就是「甜點，蜜餞，甜食」。至於餐後甜點、甜食，用 sweet 就可以，一般也常用 dessert 這個字。再看 —— sweetbread（可食用的、小牛等的）胰臟；它的味道既不 sweet，也非 bread（麵包）。

eggplant 茄子，這更奇怪了！怎麼會是 egg 的 plant 呢？它並非 egg，如果說它的果實像 egg，倒也勉強解釋的通。不過，北美的茄子是橢圓形的，取其形狀，而稱它為 eggplant 未嘗不可（台灣的茄子卻是長條形的）。

quicksand 流沙，照字面的解釋，應該是「快速移動」的沙，可是流沙卻是緩慢地移動，一點也不快速。snack bar 小吃店、coffee bar 咖啡店，bar 既是酒吧，也是小店、小吃店。怪哉！怪哉！

中文也有類似矛盾的語彙，譬如：
台灣隊打贏了日本隊。
台灣隊打敗了日本隊。
「贏」和「敗」是反義字，可是在這裡，不管打贏、打敗，都算台灣隊贏，真是莫名其妙！

諸如此類語彙的形成，雖然不按牌理出牌，但是從它矛盾的構造去透視它，也該是一種很有趣的記字方式。

發揮聯想和意會的創意能力

# 活背單字樂趣多 二部曲

## ◎ 心中永遠的痛──單字的記憶

英文單字記了又忘，忘了再記，還是拋諸腦後，好像得了失憶症一樣。到底有什麼方法可以記了不忘，又可以大量地記字呢？畢竟「單字的記憶」總是令英語學習萬般無奈。

為使讀者們能奠定記憶大量字彙的基礎，筆者淺述英文字彙的構造和記字的技巧，期望讀者們的學習，能藉此收事半功倍的效益。首先，談的是「合成字」：

## ◎ 你濃我濃──合成字

單字裡頭，最容易記憶的就是「合成字」；它常常是由兩三個簡單的字「合」起來「成」為一個字。因此，稱之為 Combining Words 或是 Compound Words。

例如 ache（疼痛）和 back、head、heart 這些簡單的字，就可以構成──

| | | | |
|---|---|---|---|
| backache | 背痛 | headache | 頭痛 |
| toothache | 牙痛 | heartache | 傷心，痛心 |
| stomachache | 胃痛 | | |

又 heart（心），加上 beat（敲擊、節拍）、break 等字，則變成──

| | | | |
|---|---|---|---|
| heartbeat | 心跳 | heartbreak | 心碎、悲傷 |
| heartbroken | 悲痛的、傷心的 | heartland | 心臟地區 |
| heartbreaking | 令人傷心的、令人悲痛的 | | |

例如 way 和 run, side, water, high 這些簡單的字，就可以構成──

| | | | |
|---|---|---|---|
| runway | 跑道，通路 | waterway | 水路 |
| sideway | 小路，旁路 | byway | 小路、旁路 |
| highway | 大道，公路 | pathway | 小路 |
| roadway | 車道 | | |

如果 way 配合字源 sub-（under之意），就變成 subway（地下鐵）。若配合 mid-（middle之意）的話，就變成了 midway（在途中的）。

以這種方式形成的字，應該不難記憶。但是也有例外——

parkway（汽車專用道，林園大道），是用來 drive（開車行走）的；可是 driveway（可通往車庫的私用車道），卻是用來 park (停車)的。豈不怪哉？

同時，語彙的形成也有「合成」的情況——

| | |
|---|---|
| foreign aid 外援 | foreign goods 外國貨 |
| foreign settlers 外僑 | foreign exchange 外匯 |

中文也有合成字的構造，例如：不+正→歪，不+好→孬，不+用→甭；那麼英文字 birthmark = 出生 + 記號→ **胎記**，至於 cutpurse = 切、割 + 錢包→ **小偷**、**扒手**，pickpocket = 挑、撿 + 口袋 →自然也是「扒手」了。

這些都是由簡短的兩三個字，合起來成為一個字的。但是，如果是比較長的兩個單字合起來，就要砍掉頭、尾，不然字就太長了。這種單字被稱為Portmanteau Word，有人譯成「混成字」，筆者將它譯成「去頭去尾合成字」，應該比較貼切一點，不信的話，您看——

**comsat** 通訊衛星 → communication 通訊、傳播 + satellite 衛星
**aerobicise** 有氧體操(運動、舞蹈) → aerobic 氧氣的 + exercise 體操
( aerobicise 也可簡稱 aerobics )
**breathalyzer** 酒測器 → breath 呼吸 + analyzer 分析/分解器
**swelegant** 非常優雅的 → swell 漂亮的、時髦的 + elegant 高雅的、優美的

根據筆者的經驗，想要大量地記住英文單字，光靠恆心與毅力是不夠的，必定得要講究記字的方法和技巧。最迅速有效的方式，就是了解單字的結構，進一步掌握它的特性，把和它相關的字眼，一口氣記起來。

發揮聯想和意會的創意能力

# 活背單字樂趣多 三部曲

**高**二那年的寒假，筆者初次接觸到一本英英字典 —— Webster's Dictionary。這本字典裏面，除了英英解釋以外，還把將近一半的英文單字，都分析出結構—**字源**。我這才知道，原來英文和中文一樣，都有部首（字源），而相同部首的字，就有相近的性質、意義。當時有此發現，我如獲至寶，便著手整理了五百個左右的字首、字根、字尾，再進一步掌握字源的特性，整組、整串地背起單字來。果然，可以迅速地記牢大量語彙。同時了解字源愈多，記憶單字的範圍就愈廣，而閱讀的速度更快。閱讀時能少查字典，更能激發學習英文的興趣。如此一來，記單字、閱讀文章，相輔相成，自然能培養出英語能力。

## ● 字尾—尾大不掉

現在就來談談「字源」——字首、字根、字尾吧！筆者先從「字尾」說起 —— 字尾 suffix，當然是放在字的尾巴了，而 suffix 這個字的構造正是：suf-，under + fix，to fasten，to fix。換句話說，是「固定在下面」，亦即「放在後面」的意思，所以 suffix 就譯成「字尾」。

舉例來說，**-ware** 便是字尾，它的定義是「器物、製成品、用具」之意，所以—

| | | | |
|---|---|---|---|
| ironware | 鐵器 | silverware | 銀器 |
| glassware | 玻璃器皿 | woodenware | 木製器具 |
| kitchenware | 廚具 | ovenware | 耐高溫的烤箱器皿 |
| tableware | 餐具 | cookware | 烹飪用具，炊具 |
| hardware | 硬體（電腦） | software | 軟體（電腦） |
| shareware = share 共享軟體 | | freeware | 免費軟體 |

又 ware 加了 s，變成 wares，即「商品、貨物」之意；ware 加上 house，變成 warehouse，則是「倉庫」了。

再看看下面這些字——

freestyle （自由式） + -er → freestyler 自由式選手
village 鄉村 + -er → villager 村民，鄉村的人
photograph 拍攝，照片 + -er → photographer 攝影師

observe 看到，觀察 + -er → observer 目擊者，觀察者，觀察員
retail 零售 + -er → retailer 零售商

在這兒字尾 **-er** 是「人」的意思，但它也有「物」的含意，例如 ──

erase 擦去，刪去 + -er → eraser 橡皮擦，黑板擦
fill  填滿 + -er → filler  填料，補白
point 指示 + -er → pointer 指針
lock  鎖  + -er → locker 鎖櫃，寄物櫃
trim  修剪 + -er → trimmer 修剪器，剪草機

但是，有個字尾 **-ster** 一般都當它是「人」的意思，可是這個「人」卻有兩種不同的意思：一是「參與…的人、和…有關的人」，一是「某種職業，某種習性的人」，而且幾乎都帶有輕視的含意。

曾經有位學生告訴我，他的英文老師教他們「中國情人節」（七夕）的英文說法是── Cowboy & Spinster Festival。我聽了之後，不禁莞爾，便回答：cowboy 是北美的牛仔（西部牛仔），spinster 在古時候是「紡織女子」的意思。spin 為「紡織」，**-ster** 在這兒則是「從事…行業的人」，卻隱含著輕視的意味。古時候，因為紡織女子的社會地位較低，所以就寫成了 spinster。但是，spinster 這個字演變到近代，變成了「年齡不小的未婚女子、老處女」的意思。Cowboy & Spinster Festival 應該譯成「西部牛仔和老處女的節日」，怎會是牛郎織女節呢？

西洋情人節是 Saint Valentine's Day。中國情人節可以套用西洋的說法，將之改成 Chinese Valentine's Day 即可。若要符合七夕的由來，依它的故事背景，則可說成 Cowherd & Weaving Maid（Girl）Festival。因為 cowherd 是「牧牛者」，是 cow 牛，加上 **-herd**「放牧」之意，又好比 shepherd、goatherd 是「牧羊者」，是 sheep 或 goat 羊的放牧者；herdsman 或 herder 則是「牧人」。

字尾 **-er** 和 **-ster** 雖然都有「人」的意思，但 **-er** 指的是一般的人，而 **-ster** 則有「不怎麼樣的人」而帶有輕蔑的味道。例如──

gang 幫派     + -ster → gangster 歹徒，匪徒
game 遊戲     + -ster → gamester 賭徒，賭棍
trick 欺騙     + -ster → trickster 騙子
old  老的     + -ster → oldster 老傢伙，老年人
pun  使用雙關語 + -ster → punster 好用雙關語的人

ring 壞人集團　　　　　+ -ster → ringster 結黨營私者，黨徒
poll 民意測驗（調查）+ -ster → pollster 民意測驗（調查）家

● 最初剛有民意測驗（調查）時，既不客觀、又不公正，無法取得人們信任，所以造字者便把他 **-ster**一下，造出 pollster 這個字來。

同時，從字尾也可以判斷單字的屬性，像 **-ify**、**-ize** 結尾的字必是動詞。例如—

| | | | |
|---|---|---|---|
| simplify | 使簡化 | qualify | 使合格 |
| organize | 組織 | specialize | 專攻 |

**-en** 也可當作動詞的字尾，例字如下：

| | | | |
|---|---|---|---|
| lengthen | 使長，加長 | widen | 使變寬，擴大 |
| strengthen | 加強，使變強 | weaken | 變弱，削弱 |
| heighten | 提高，增高 | deepen | 使加深，變深 |

**en-** 也可以是動詞的字首，例如：

| | | | | |
|---|---|---|---|---|
| encourage | 鼓勵，激發 | → en-, to make + courage | 勇氣 | |
| enforce | 執行，實施，強加於… | → en-, to make + force | 力量，迫使 | |
| enfeeble | 使衰弱，使無力 | → en-, to make + feeble | 虛弱的，無力的 | |
| enrage | 使憤怒，激怒 | → en-, to make + rage | 憤怒 | |
| entrap | 誘捕，使上當 | → en-, to make + trap | 陷阱，圈套 | |

循此規律性來記單字，想要迅速記牢大量的語彙，簡直是易如反掌折枝！
好啦！各位看倌，筆者絮絮叨叨了許久，也累了，且讓筆者擱筆品茗歇息一下吧！

發揮聯想和意會的創意能力

# 活背單字樂趣多 四部曲

撰文 / 高志豪

## 本是同 根 生

「字根」是英文單字的根本、語彙的源頭。要是能記上百來個字根的話,拿它們來記生字,短時間內,便可牢記一萬個以上的英文單字。同時,也不會忘卻這些單字的中文意義。舉一些實例吧!

## flex

flex 這個字根的意思是 to bend(彎曲),所以——

**flex<u>ible</u>** → *flex*, to bend + *-ible*, able to = able to bend　a. 易彎曲的,彈性的,柔順的

**in<u>flex</u>ible** → *in-*, not + *flex*, to bend + *-ible*, able to = not able to bend　a. 不易彎曲的,堅定的,不屈的

**re<u>flex</u>** → *re-*, back + *flex*, to bend = to bend back　v. 使反射(折回);n. 反映,反射作用

**bendable** 也是 able to bend 的構造,所以是 **flexible** 的同義字;又而 **unbendable** → *un-*, not + *bend*, to bend + *-able*, able to = not able to bend,文字結構和 inflexible 一模一樣,所以 unbendable 和 inflexible 是同義字。

## mort

字根 mort 是 death(死亡)、dead(死亡)之意,所以——

**<u>mort</u>al** → *mort*, death, dead + -al, of = dead;mortal「致命的,不免一死的」,這和 deadly 的意思一樣。

**im<u>mort</u>al** → *im-* = *in-*, not + *mort*, death, dead + -al, of = not dead;immortal 自然是「不死的,永生的」了。

## rupt

rupt 這個字根的定義是 break(破裂)、burst(爆裂),故——

**bankrupt** → *bank*, bank（銀行）+ *rupt*, to break = to break bank，所以 bankrupt 是 a. 破產的、 n. 破產者

**corrupt** → *cor-*, together + *rupt*, to break = to break together（一起破爛），corrupt 是 a. 腐敗的、貪污的

**disrupt** → *dis-*, apart + *rupt*, to break = to break apart（裂開），disrupt 是 v. 使分裂、使破裂

**interrupt** → *inter-*, between + *rupt*, to break = to break between（在…之間破裂），interrupt 是 v. 打斷、使中斷、打擾。

又**erupt** → *e-*, out + *rupt*, to break = to break out, 所以 **outbreak**、**outburst**、**break out**、**burst out** 的構造和 **erupt** 相同，自然都具有「爆發」的意思了。

## nov

字根 nov 是 new 的意思，因此形成——

**innovate** → *in-*, in + *nov*, new + *-ate*, to make = to make new (in), innovate 是 v. 改革、發明、創始。

**nova** → *nov*, new + *-a*（名詞字尾），nova 即是 n. 新星。

**novice** → *nov*, new + *-ice*（名詞字尾），novice 就成了 n. 新手、生手，和 **beginner** 一樣的意思，而 beginner = begin(n) + *-er*, man。

**renovate** → *re-*, again + *nov*, new + *-ate*, to make = to make new again，所以 renovate 是 v. 革新、使變新。

　　從以上所舉的這些例子，你可以看出字根是字源（英文部首）的一種，它的位置或在前、或在後、或在中間，雖然游移不定，可是就這三個位置而已。英文的字源比起中文的部首，可就簡單多了。且看看中文的部首如何——梟、鷺、鴃、鵬、鳳，這五個漢字全屬「鳥」字部，分別在「上、下、左、右、中」五個位置。那麼，請問：「鳥」這個部首，什麼時候該擺在上面（下面、左邊、右邊、中間）呢？誰能解開筆者的疑惑？

# 五百年前是一家

筆者閒來無事，喜歡研究英文字彙的結構，玩一些文字遊戲，也常拿英文單字和漢字作比較，每每有意外發現，而暗自竊喜！

譬如：「侖」這個漢字，在字典裡屬「人」字旁，換句話說，它的部首是「人」。「侖」是一個字，不是部首，而它的意義是──

　　侖ㄌㄨㄣˊ者，條理層次也。

那麼，請看──「倫」理、言「論」、「掄」元、滿腹經「綸」、風水「輪」流轉，其中「倫、論、掄、綸、輪」是不是都具有「條理層次」的含意？「侖」，在這兒是否可以當作「部首」使用？可是，中文並沒有「侖」這個部首，奇怪不？

英文單字的構造也有這種情形，有一些結構根本不是字源（部首），卻可以賦予特定的意義，也具有字源（部首）的功能。例如 **nnel** 出現在單字的尾端時，那個字就有「管路、通道」的含意──

| | | | |
|---|---|---|---|
| cha**nnel** | 海峽，頻道 | chu**nnel** | 水底列車隧道 |
| fu**nnel** | 排氣管，漏斗，煙囪 | ke**nnel** | 排水溝，溝渠 |
| ru**nnel** | 小河，水溝 | tu**nnel** | 隧道，地道 |

這些字不是都有「管路、通道」的意思嗎？可是 **nnel** 並不是所謂的字首、字尾、字根啊！

又 **str** 並非字首，但它擺在單字前頭的時候，常常造成那些單字具有「緊張、壓力、用力；直，線條」的意思──

| | | | |
|---|---|---|---|
| **str**ain | *v.* 使緊張；*n.* 緊張，壓力 | **str**angle | *v.* 扼殺，使窒息 |
| **str**engthen | *v.* 加強，使強 | **str**enuous | *a.* 費力的，用力的 |
| **str**ess | *v.* 重讀；*n.* 壓力，強調 | **str**ive | *v.* 努力，抗爭 |
| **str**aight | *a.* 直的；*n.* 直線部分 | **str**eamline | *a.* 流線型的 |
| **str**eak | *n.* 線條，條紋 | **str**iped | *a.* 有條紋的 |

**dr** 起頭的字，有不少是和「水」有關的——

| | | | |
|---|---|---|---|
| <u>dr</u>ip = droplet | *n.* 小水滴 | <u>dr</u>ain | *v.* 漸次排水 |
| <u>dr</u>ench | *v.* 浸透；*n.* 大雨，豪雨 | <u>dr</u>ift | *v.* 漂流 |
| <u>dr</u>ibble | *v.* 流口水，涓滴 | <u>dr</u>izzle | *v.* 下細雨（毛毛雨） |
| <u>dr</u>ool | *v.* 流口水，垂涎 | <u>dr</u>ip-dry | *v.* 隨洗隨乾；*a.* 隨洗隨乾的 |
| <u>dr</u>oughty | *a.* 乾旱的，缺雨水的 | <u>dr</u>own | *v.* 淹死，溺斃 |

　　**nnel**、**str**、**dr** 這一類非字源的構造，筆者稱之為 Special Word-element（特殊字彙結構）。它們就算不是部首，和部首不是老鄉，恐怕在五百年前和字源也是一家吧！

# 閱讀篇
*TOEIC 閱讀即戰力*

## 分類的閱讀

新版多益測驗閱讀部份的 Part 7 中，單篇文章的閱讀測驗大約考八至十篇文章，考生回答二十八個問題；而雙篇閱讀的閱讀測驗，則考生須看完四組的兩篇文章五個問題，共有八篇文章、二十個問題。總計閱讀測驗的部份，大約是十六至十八篇文章、四十八道題目。在七十五分鐘之內，要答完句子填空四十題、短文克漏字十二題（三或四篇文章），再加上單、雙篇閱讀，這「份量」對欠缺閱讀經驗的考生，未免太沉重了！然而，如何減輕這沉重的負擔呢？那得靠養成不斷地閱讀的習慣才行！

國人的英語學習，多半只重逐字逐句的文法解析和翻譯，傾向死氣沉沉而被動的閱讀方式——就是要有老師講解一句，才懂一句。這樣就算完全看懂了，充其量也只是 sophomore（半瓶醋、半壺水）。殊不知閱讀的樂趣可以從主動的閱讀中獲得，進而增進我們的理解力——就是讓文章、書本直接引領我們！

筆者就此簡單地來談一下「分類的閱讀」——藉著閱讀養成邏輯思考的能力，和判定文章屬性的知覺。

一般閱讀文章可分成五類，即 Question-Answer Pattern（問答型）、Opinion-Reason Pattern（意見理由型）、Substantiated Facts Pattern（證實事實型）、Sharing Experience Pattern（分享經驗型）、Imparting Information Pattern（告知資訊型）。筆者——說明如下——

### ● 問答型 (Question-Answer Pattern)

此類文章通常在標題或第一段開始，作者便擺明了所要討論的問題，敘述問題癥結所在。接著，便自問自答，討論解決之道，或只說明問題發生的原因、現象，讓讀者去思考解決的方法。例如底下這篇短文——

Which is more valuable? To provide a $100,000 heart transplant for an ailing child of indigent parents? Or to use that money for prenatal care that may enhance the life expectancy of fetuses being carried by 120 expectant mothers? Surely the leader of the democratic capitalist world can afford both. Yet a growing number of health experts argue that the most developed countries, in fact, no longer has the financial resources to provide unlimited medical treatment for all those who need it. The only solution, they say, is rationing health care.

哪一種較有價值？為貧窮父母的生病小孩，提供十萬美元的心臟移植手術？或者，把同樣的金錢花在產前照顧，而可能提高一百二十位孕婦對胎兒生命的期待？當然，民主的資本主義世界的領導者，有能力負擔以上這兩者。但是，愈來愈多的醫療保健專家認為：事實上，大多數已開發國家，不再有財力提供給所有需要的人無限制的醫療照顧。他們表示：唯一的解決之道，就是定額分配的醫療保健。

| [單字] | | |
|---|---|---|
| valuable | a. | 有價值的，有用的 |
| transplant | n. | 移植 |
| ailing | a. | 生病的 |
| indigent | a. | 貧窮的 |
| prenatal | a. | 產前的 |
| expectancy | n. | 期待，期望 |
| fetus = foetus | n. | 胎兒 |
| expectant | a. | 即將生孩子的 |
| capitalist | n. | 資本家 |
| afford | v. | 能堪，提供，付得起 |
| unlimited | a. | 無限制的 |
| treatment | n. | 治療，待遇 |
| solution | n. | 解決(方法) |
| rationing | v. | 定量分配 |

Which is more valuable ... expectant mother? 便是作者點出的問題。至於解決之道,則作者提出專家們的意見:rationing health care。

關於健康保險的醫療制度,一向是各國政府芒刺在背的棘手問題;是該站在人道的立場考量呢?還是顧慮健保照護的合理性、公平性?這是值得看完以上這篇短文的讀者們深思的一個問題。若看完後,不加思索,則只能增加我們的資訊,卻不能增進個人的思考和理解力。即使是閱讀八卦新聞(gossip news),也該作一番思考才對。

## ● 意見理由型 (Opinion-Reason Pattern)

1998年,美國總統Bill Clinton和白宮女實習生 Monica Lewinsky「轟動武林、驚動萬教」的性醜聞(sex scandal)曝光之後,在司法調查和共和黨提出的彈劾案下,Clinton 雖然「滿面豆花」,卻也驚險過關,未被定罪,這是史上有名的 Zippergate(拉鍊門醜聞)。此一事件中,Clinton 總統以一場簡短而令人動容的電視演說,為這件不光彩而煽情的醜聞,劃下了休止符。且讓我們欣賞一下這篇精彩的演說詞 ——

### Clinton's Speech to American Public

"Good evening. This afternoon in this room, from this chair, I testified before the Office of Independent Counsel and the grand jury.

| [單字] | testify | **v.** 作證,證實 |
| --- | --- | --- |
| | Independent Counsel | (美)獨立檢察官 |
| | grand jury | 大陪審團 |

"I answered their questions truthfully, including questions about my private life, questions no American citizen would ever want to answer.

"Still, I must take complete responsibility for all my actions, both public and private. And that is why I am speaking to you tonight.

| [筆者按] | 美國人最忌諱去探人隱私 ( personal privacy ),Clinton 則表示願意回答有關私生活的問題,且又肯負責。 |
| --- | --- |

"As you know, in a deposition in January, I was asked questions about my relationship with Monica Lewinsky. While my answers were legally accurate, I did not volunteer information.

"Indeed, I did have a relationship with Miss Lewinsky that was not appropriate. In fact, it was wrong. It constituted a critical lapse in judgment and a personal failure on my part for which I am solely and completely responsible.

| [單字] | deposition | *n.* 證詞，宣誓作證 |
|---|---|---|
| | volunteer | *v.* 主動提供(資訊) |
| | critical | *a.* 非常重要的，吹毛求疵的 |
| | lapse | *n.* 過失，疏忽，行為失檢 |
| | failure | *n.* 失敗 |

[筆者按]　這段話的意思是說：我只是沒有主動提供檢察官資料而已，在法律上，我還是站得住腳的。我和 Lewinsky 的關係，可說是「不恰當」(有什麼大不了的！)。嘿，不對，不對！只是觀念上有嚴重過失，是我個人的失敗啦！

"But I told the grand jury today and I say to you now that at no time did I ask anyone to lie, to hide or destroy evidence or to take any other unlawful action. I know that my public comments and my silence about this matter gave a false impression. I misled people, including even my wife. I deeply regret that.

| [單字] | mislead | *v.* 誤導 |
|---|---|---|

[筆者按]　這段話意味著：我沒有要別人撒謊、隱藏或摧毀證據，或者採取不法行動 (是我自己撒謊…)。我公開的談話也好、沉默也好，都會造成你們錯誤的印象 (你們真的不好「款待」)。我深深地 regret (遺憾)。但是我絕對不講 I'm very sorry for that. 或者 I sincerely apologize for that. 因為這件事情沒那麼嚴重嘛！

"I can only tell you I was motivated by many factors. First, by a desire to protect myself from the embarrassment of my own conduct.

"I was also very concerned about protecting my family. The fact that these questions were being asked in a politically inspired lawsuit, which has since been dismissed, was a consideration, too.

| [單字] | motivate | *v.* 激起，促使 |
|---|---|---|
| | conduct | *n.* 行為，處理方式 |
| | inspired | *a.* 被激起/喚起的 |
| | lawsuit | *n.* (非刑事案件的)訴訟 |
| | dismiss | *v.* 駁回，不受理 |

| [筆者按] | 這段話的意思是：我撒謊，是因為不願意受困窘嘛！我還顧慮到家人呢！（我的老婆 Hillary Clinton 可不好惹的！）還有，這絕對是政治化的訴訟造成的(可能是政治迫害)！ |
|---|---|

"In addition, I had real and serious concerns about an independent counsel investigation that began with private business dealings 20 years ago, dealings I might add about which an independent federal agency found no evidence of any wrongdoing by me or my wife over two years ago.

"The independent counsel investigation moved on to my staff and friends, then into my private life. And now the investigation itself is under investigation.

| [單字] | business dealings | 商業交易，商務關係 |
|---|---|---|
| | federal agency | 聯邦機構 |
| | wrongdoing | *n.* 違法，犯罪 |
| | move on to | 轉向 |

| [筆者按] | 這段話牽扯到過往的 Whitewatergate（白水門醜聞）：那該死的獨立檢察官 Kenneth Starl！他從1994年起，就開始調查我擁有50%股份的 Whitewater Department Corporation，說什麼官商勾結啦，妨礙司法、作偽證啦！還好，當時上帝正在睡覺，Starl 找不到確切的證據。但是，天殺的，該死！他轉向調查我的員工，甚至於私生活咧！Starl 調查了幾年，花了近千萬美元的公帑， |
|---|---|

> 耗費鉅大的社會成本，他的調查報告和資料堆滿了好幾個房
> 間！他現在也在被調查是否過度浪費民脂民膏。活該！該死
> 的 Kenneth Starl！

"This has gone on too long, cost too much and hurt too many innocent people.

"Now, this matter is between me, the two people I love most – my wife and our daughter – and our God. I must put it right, and I am prepared to do whatever it takes to do so.

"Nothing is more important to me personally. But it is private, and I intend to reclaim my family life for my family. It's nobody's business but ours.

| [單字] | reclaim | *v.* 重得，取回 |
|---|---|---|

| [筆者按] | 這段話的意思是：這件八卦也扯太久了。可不要因為我是美國總統，就緊追不放，還累及無辜！這是我的私事，不干別人的閒事哪！ |
|---|---|

"Even presidents have private lives. It is time to stop the pursuit of personal destruction and the prying into private lives and get on with our national life.

"Our country has been distracted by this matter for too long, and I take my responsibility for my part in all of this. That is all I can do.

| [單字] | pry | *v.* 刺探，打聽 |
|---|---|---|
| | distract | *v.* 使分心(分散注意力) |

| [筆者按] | 雖然我是總統，也有私生活啊！你們不要被這件緋聞，噢，不對！不要被「不恰當的關係」的閒話，分散了注意力！當然，我是該負全責的啦！ |
|---|---|

"Now it is time – in fact, it is past time to move on.

"We have important work to do – real opportunities to seize, real problems to solve, real security matters to face.

| [單字] | move on | 繼續前進；變換(話題或工作) |
|--------|---------|---------------------------|

| [筆者按] | 這是換個話題的時候了！我們有正事要辦、有問題等著解決、有安全問題要面對吧！ |
|----------|----------------------------------------------------------------|

"And so tonight, I ask you to turn away from the spectacle of the past seven months, to repair the fabric of our national discourse, and to return our attention to all the challenges and all the promise of the next American century.

Thank you for watching. And good night."

| [單字] | spectacle | **n.** 異常的事/現象 |
|--------|-----------|---------------------|
| | fabric | **n.** 結構 |
| | discourse | **n.** 交談 |
| | promise | **n.** 前途，希望 |

| [筆者按] | 今晚，就拜託各位換個話題吧！我們必須轉移注意力到下一個美國人的世紀的挑戰和願景，這才對嘛！ |
|----------|----------------------------------------------------------------|
| [筆者按] | 這段話讓筆者回想起求學時代的演講或作文，在結尾的時候，都必然加上：我們要處變不驚、慎謀能斷，然後自立自強，進一步反攻大陸，拯救大陸同胞於水深火熱之中！ |

　　讀者們，看完這篇演說詞，您有何感想呢？您可知道：當時 Clinton 的民調支持度，已低落到百分之三十左右。然而，從電視上看到他初始以和緩低沉的語調，然後似乎愧疚又帶著辯解意味的言語，進而轉為鏗鏘有力、鼓舞人們奮發的言詞，這堪稱是一場精采絕倫的表演。在 Clinton 電視演說之後，他的民調支持度居然遽升到百分之六十五左右；而以此醜聞猛烈抨擊他的共和黨，在1998年期中選舉中卻敗下陣來。美國人的天真幼稚( naive )於此可見，令人為之搖頭。

　　這篇演講稿裡，充斥著 I tell ...、I say ...、 that is why ...、 as you know ...、I know ...、I had concerns about ...、I take ...、I ask you ... 諸如此類的字眼，都是要陳述自己的意見、看法、理由，這是標準的 Opinion-Reason Pattern；同時，從

下其他的文字也可以看出來，如 I think ...、I believe ...、I prefer ...、I judge ...、I regard ...、I sure ...、as I see it ...、in my opinion ...、according to my viewpoint ...等等，這些都是「意見理由型」的文章經常出現的字眼。

## ● 證實事實型（Substantiated Facts Pattern）

這一類型的文章，開宗明義以「文章主旨（結論）」作為開頭，再列舉事實，證明「主旨（結論）」的可信度和可靠性；同時，作者引用資料、科學觀察及實驗等例證，和「意見理由型」（Opinion-Reason Pattern）明顯不同，而在「證實事實型」的文章中沒有人稱代名詞，沒有 I think ...、I believe ...等的字眼。試舉一篇範文於下——

---

**New from science: a technique to extract DNA from 20,000-year-old dung.**

It can't be used to create extinct creatures like Hollywood scientists do with DNA in dinosaur movies, but it may solve mysteries about animals now gone forever. "This is not 'Jurassic Park'," said Hendrik N. Poinar, a University of Munich researcher. Poinar, a molecular biologist, led a team that discovered a chemical agent that will extract from ancient dung DNA fragments that come from the animal and from the food it ate. The researchers, reporting Friday in the journal Science, said the technique has been used on dung from a giant American ground sloth that disappeared from the fossil record about 11,000 years ago. The dung was found in a Gypsum Cave in Nevada and was age dated at about 20,000 years.

---

**科學新知：從兩萬年前的糞便萃取DNA的技術。**

這種技術無法像恐龍電影中，好萊塢的科學家們處理DNA一樣，用於創造絕種的動物。但是，它可能解開永遠消失的動物之謎。「這不是『侏儸紀公園』！」Hendrik N. Poinar 表示，他是慕尼黑大學的研究人員。Poniar 是一位分子生物學家，領導一個團隊，發現一種化學劑，能夠從年代久遠的糞便中，萃取來自動物

和牠所吃的食物的DNA碎片。在星期五的「科學」期刊，研究學者們報導：這項技術一直被用在美洲棲息洞穴的巨大的樹獺的糞便。從化石紀錄看來，牠在一萬一千年前就消失了。這糞便在內華達州的一個「石膏岩洞」中被發現，大約存在兩萬年了。

| [單字] | | | |
|---|---|---|---|
| | technique | *n.* | 方法，技術 |
| | extract | *v.* | 抽出，萃取 |
| | dung | *a.* | （大型動物之）糞便 |
| | extinct | *n.* | 絕種的，消失的，滅絕的 |
| | dinosaur | *n.* | 恐龍 |
| | mystery | *n.* | 謎，不可思議之事物 |
| | Jurassic Park | | 侏儸紀公園 |
| | molecular biologist | | 分子生物專家 |
| | agent | *n.* | 劑，因素 |
| | fragment | *n.* | 碎片，殘存部份 |
| | sloth | *n.* | 樹獺（產於中南美洲） |
| | fossil | *n.* | 化石 |

「證實事實型」的文章性質，泰半傾向於科學研究和科學事實的報導，而佐以數據、分析，沒有冗言贅語。請您再看下面一文，係摘錄自2007年12月11日美聯社的一篇報導：

An already relentless melting of the Arctic greatly accelerated this summer, a warning sign that some scientists worry could mean global warming has passed an ominous tipping point. One even speculated that summer sea ice would be gone in five years.

北極原已融冰不斷，今年夏天更加速融冰了。有些科學家憂心忡忡：這個警訊可能意味著全球暖化已經出現了不祥的凶兆。一位科學家甚至猜測，夏天的海面冰層會在五年內消失。

| [單字] | | | |
|---|---|---|---|
| | relentless | *a.* | 不間斷的，無休止的 |
| | melt | *v.* | 融化，消失 |
| | the Arctic | | 北極，北極區 |

Greenland's ice sheet melted nearly 19 billion tons more than the previous high mark, and the volume of Arctic sea ice at summer's end was half what it was just four years earlier, according to new NASA satellite data obtained by the Associated Press.

"The Arctic is screaming," said Mark Serreze, senior scientist at the **gocernment's** snow and ice data center in Boulder, Colo.

Just last year, two top scientists surprised their colleagues by projecting that the Arctic sea ice was melting so rapidly that it could disappear entirely by the summer of 2040.

This week, after reviewing his own new data, NASA climate scientist Jay Zwally said: "At this rate, the Arctic Ocean could be nearly ice-free at the end of summer by 2012, much faster than previous predictions."

美聯社獲得的美國航空總署新的衛星資料顯示：格陵蘭冰帽的融化，比先前的最高紀錄多出幾近190億噸。同時，在今年夏天結束時，北極的海面冰層只剩下四年前的一半。

「北極正在吶喊！」科羅拉多州 Boulder 的國家冰雪資料中心資深研究員Mark Serreze，這麼說道。

就在去年，有兩位頂尖的科學家，提出令他們同僚吃驚的推測：北極的海面冰層融化速度太快了，可能到2040年夏天，就會完全消失。

本週，美國航空總署的氣候研究員 Jay Zwally，在看過新資料以後表示：「照這樣下去，北極海洋可能到2012年夏天結束時，就幾乎沒有冰層了。這要比先前預測的快得多了！

So scientists in recent days have been asking themselves these questions: Was the record melt seen all over the Arctic in 2007 a blip amid relentless and steady warming? Or has everything sped up to a new climate cycle that goes beyond the worst-case scenarios presented by computer models?

所以，近來科學家們一直問自己這些問題：在2007年，整個北極冰層融化的紀錄，只是持續不斷而穩定的暖化現象的一個小問題嗎？或者是全球已加速進入新的氣候週期，遠超過電腦模擬所能呈現的最壞的可能情況？

誠然，只要看過美國前副總統 Gore 的 An Inconvenient Truth（不願面對的真相），您就知道人類已將地球蹧躂得快要覓無淨土了。即使美國總統 Obama 在他二〇〇九年的勝選演說中，都要提到：

Even as we celebrate tonight, we know the challenges that tomorrow will bring are the greatest of our lifetime—two wars, a planet in peril, the worst financial crisis in a century.

即使今晚慶功，我們也知道明天將面臨的是這輩子最大的挑戰：兩場戰爭，一是瀕危的地球，一是百年僅見的最糟的金融危機。

a planet in peril 簡單四個字控訴著人類的罪惡，也道盡人們心中的沉痛！看完美聯社的這段報導，豈能不心有戚戚嗎？

## ● 告知資訊型（Imparting Information Pattern）

Thomas L. Friedman 繼2005年出版了 The World Is Flat (世界是平的)之後，於2008年又推出 Hot, Flat, and Crowded (世界又熱、又平、又擠)的大作，全書主旨放在 Why We Need A Green Revolution — And How It Can Renew America。他平實的寫作風格，卻處處透露警世的機鋒。他認為應該以綠化作為國家安全和經濟利益的核心；人類無法不正視日益嚴重的生態破壞、氣候暖化的問題，而應以**綠能革命**（Green Revolution），作為全球的**綠色行動規範**（Code Green）。

筆者試著摘譯 **Hot, Flat, and Crowded** 一書中的一小段，供作讀者們參考，該篇提到歐洲小國丹麥以課稅的方式，使能源更加昂貴，促使民眾節約能源，進而提升能源效率。同時，提供讀者們丹麥藉此措施創新能源的資訊：

Premium gasoline in Denmark in 2008 was about $9 a gallon. On top of that, Denmark has a CO2 tax, which it put in place in the mid-1990s to promote efficiency, even though it had discovered offshore oil by then. "When you get your electricity bill you see your CO2 tax [itemized]," the minister said. Surely all of this killed the Danish economy, right? Guess again. "Since 1981 our economy has grown 70 percent, while our energy consumption has been kept almost flat all those years," she said. Unemployment is a little less than 2 percent. And Denmark's early emphasis on solar and wind power, which now provide 16 percent of its total energy consumption, spawned a whole new export industry.

在2008年，丹麥的高級汽油價格每加崙約9美元。此外，還有二氧化碳稅。這是在90年代裡，丹麥已發現了近海石油，但為了提高能源效率而開徵的稅。「當你收到電費帳單時，你會看到列舉的二氧化碳稅的項目。」部長 Connie Hedegaurd 這麼說。當然，這項措施重創了丹麥的經濟。是嗎？猜猜看！「從1981年以來，我們經濟已成長了70%，而能源消耗量在這些年卻幾乎沒有變化。」她說著。失業率則略少於2%，同時，丹麥早就把重點放在太陽能和風力發電。這提供它目前能源總消耗量的16%，也創造出整個的新的出口產業。

| [單字] | premium | | ***a.*** 高品質的，高價的 |
| --- | --- | --- | --- |
| | on top of | | 除…之外 |
| | efficiency | | ***n.*** 效率，效能 |
| | offshore | | ***a.*** 近海的，境外的 |
| | itemized | | ***a.*** 逐項列舉的 |
| | consumption | | ***n.*** 消耗，消耗量 |
| | flat | | ***a.*** 平的，無變化的 |
| | emphasis | | ***n.*** 重點，重心，重要性 |
| | solar | | ***a.*** 太陽的 |
| | spawn | | ***v.*** 造成，引發；產（卵） |

底下再介紹一篇短文，摘錄自 Elizabeth C. Economy 在 Foreign Affairs（2007年9月7日—10月7日）發表的文章。

China's leaders plan to relocate 400 million people — equivalent to well over the entire population of the United States — to newly developed urban centers between 2000 and 2030. In the process, they will erect half of all the buildings expected to be constructed in the world during that period. This is a troubling prospect considering that Chinese buildings are not energy efficient — in fact, they are roughly two and a half times less so than those in Germany. Furthermore, newly urbanized Chinese, who use air conditioners, televisions, and refrigerators, consume about three and a half times more energy than do their rural counterparts.

中國領導人計劃在2000年到2030年之間，將四億人口遷移到新開發的都會中心，相當於遠超過了美國人口總數。在這個過程中，他們將興建全世界預計在這段期間內要蓋的大樓數量的一半。一想到中國的高樓大廈並無節能功效，就令人憂慮。

事實上，它們的能源效率大約比德國低兩倍半。此外，新近都市化的中國人，他們使用空調設備、電視機和電冰箱，所消耗的能源比鄉村的人多了三倍半。

看到這裡，筆者心中百味雜陳，萌生和 Friedman 一樣的疑問：What exactly does it look like when crowded meets flat? 當它（世界）變平又變擠時，到底是什麼樣子？

「現代化」的結果，可能造成地球萬劫不復？科技的突飛猛進，帶給人類的是福？或是禍？這真是值得我們省思的問題！

## ● 分享經驗型（Sharing Experience Pattern）

以下兩個段落是摘錄自 Alice Schroeder 著的 THE SNOWBALL — Warren Buffett and the Business of Life 中的文字，若將它們視作短文來看的話，應當是屬於 Sharing Experience Pattern（分享經驗型），因為全是 Warren Buffett 的現身說法，將自己的體驗、心得說出，與他人分享，所以此類型的文章，經常是作者的經驗之談，也常以第一人稱的口吻敘述。

If you are going to drive 10,000-pound trucks across a bridge repeatedly, it is well to build one that can withstand 15,000-pound loads rather than one that can withstand 10,001 pounds ... It is a big mistake to have lots of financial obligations and no cash reserve ... Personally, I have never used more than twenty-five percent borrowed money in my life, including when I had only $10,000 and had ideas that made me wish I had $1,000,000.

如果你要開10,000磅重的卡車一再過橋的話，那最好建造一座能承受15,000磅重量的橋，而不是禁得起10,001磅重的橋⋯負債累累又身無分文，這是一大錯誤⋯就我個人而言，我這輩子的花用，沒有一筆有超過25%向人借來的。這包括了當

我只有一萬美元，而某些妄想使我希望賺得一百萬元的時候，也是如此。

誠然，Buffett 就如同他的一位朋友形容他的：He never does anything that isn't a win for him.（他絕對不做他不會贏的事情。）所以，他不躁進，也不保守，因此累積了驚人的財富。

I don't enjoy battles. I won't run from them if I need to do it, but I don't enjoy them at all. When it came to the board, Charlie and I didn't even vote against it. We voted yes. We didn't even abstain, because abstaining is the same thing as throwing down the gauntlet. And there were other things at Salomon. One thing after another would come up that I thought was nutty, but they didn't want me to say anything. And then the question is, do you say anything? I don't get in fights just to get in fights.

　　我不喜歡爭論。如果必須這麼做的時候，我不會逃避，不過我一點也不喜歡爭論。當董事會產生爭論時，我和查理不會投票反對，我們投贊成票。我們不會放棄投票，因為放棄投票，就如同向人提出挑戰。「所羅門」有其他別的事情，我認為瘋狂的事情一件件跟著來（註）。但是，他們不要我說什麼。然後接著問題來了：你說什麼？我才不會為了抗爭而抗爭。（註）「所羅門」為債券公司，其針對客戶需求，提供各種不同的債券。

這就是 Buffett 處理「爭論」的態度，不會為了抗爭而抗爭的哲學。他從麵包店、雜貨店打工，在耶誕節也送報…日積月累，小心謹慎地滾動「雪球」，同時一

He wasn't looking backward to the top of the hill. It was a big world, and he was just starting out.

　　閱讀文章的類型大致可分成以上五種粗淺的分類，至於閱讀能力的提升，就是要不斷地閱讀、閱讀、閱讀！閱讀習慣的養成，才是所有學習語文的關鍵！

*TOEIC* 閱讀即戰力

# 閱讀文章的四種層次

1972年問世的增訂版〝**How To Read A Book**〞，是由 **Mortimer J. Adler** 和 **Charles Van Doren** 大幅改寫 Adler 在1940年的舊作而成。筆者參考了 How To Read A Book 增訂版的內容，依循其綱要，再融合個人的學習經驗和心得，才落筆成就本文——**閱讀文章的四種層次**。

Adler 和 Van Doren 在書中所提到的第四層次的閱讀叫作 Syntopical Reading（綜合主題閱讀），也可說是 Comparative Reading（比較閱讀）；這種層次的閱讀，得要就同一主題參閱很多書籍，不能只看一本書，而且要分析、比較各書主題的相關內容。然而，英語閱讀能力若要達到如此境界，可不是一年半載就辦得到的。至於 How To Read A Book 一書，是兩位作者寫給美國人看的，對於母語不是英語的我們，若想強化 **TOEIC** 的閱讀能力，應該只要要求自己達到第三、至少第二層次的閱讀就可以了。

如果把 How To Read A Book 改成 **How To Read An Essay**（or A Paragraph），或許更實際一點。那麼就不要好高騖遠，讓筆者來談談「如何閱讀一篇文章（或段落）」吧！

● **第一層次的閱讀——** Basic Reading 基礎閱讀

**What does the word mean?**
**What does the sentence say?**

這是初步閱讀的人經常提出的問題，甚至有些人從小到大，至少學了十年的英文，還總是將這兩句掛在嘴上。

奇怪的是：**為什麼不自己動手查字典？或上網查閱資料？**

筆者在南陽街教授 TOEFL、GRE、SAT 等留學英語的時候，經常碰到這種把老師當成字典、電腦的學生，筆者在回答他（她）的問題時，心中卻總是納悶：難道字典擺在書架上，只是為了妝點門面、冒充斯文？電腦和網路只是利用來玩電子遊

或交友聯誼？

　　「勤」查字典、「勤」找資料，這是「第一層次的閱讀──基礎閱讀」的時候，應該具備的學習英語的認知和能力。就拿底下幾個例子來說吧！可以依照下列順序來學習：

**瀏覽全句→查閱單字→細思句意→了解句意**（練習翻譯）

It's crazy to take little in-between jobs just because they look good on your résumé. (註1)

只為了要讓履歷表好看，便去做些過渡性質的差事，這是不切實際的。

| | | |
|---|---|---|
| crazy | *a.* | 不切實際的 |
| in-between | *a.* | 居中的，過渡的 |
| résumé | *n.* | 履歷表 |

Theoretically the oceans could have sustained life-forms that looked like this. (註2)

理論上，海洋中可能存在這樣的生物。

| | | |
|---|---|---|
| theoretically | *adv.* | 理論上存在 |
| sustain | *v.* | 維持，支撐 |
| life-form | *n.* | 生物（= life form） |

Scientists refer to what has been happening in the earth's atmosphere over the past century as the "enhanced greenhouse effect". (註3)

科學家們以「高溫室效應」，來說明過去一世紀以來地球的大氣層發生的情況。

| | | |
|---|---|---|
| refer to | | 說到，提起 |
| atmosphere | *n.* | 大氣，大氣層 |
| enhanced | *a.* | 增強的，提高的 |
| greenhouse effect | | 溫室效應 |

When my breakfast arrived I opened my briefcase and pulled out some notes I'd taken the prior night before I'd hit the sack. (註4)

早餐送來時，我打開公事包，拿出昨晚睡前寫的一些筆記。

| | | |
|---|---|---|
| briefcase | *n.* | 公事包 |
| prior | *a.* | 先前的，事先的 |
| hit the sack | | 睡覺，就寢 |
| | | （ = sack out, sack in ） |

Limited love asks for possession of the beloved, but the unlimited asks only for itself. (註5)

狹窄的愛，要求佔有愛人；而無限的愛，只要求愛的本身。

| | | |
|---|---|---|
| limited | *a.* | 有限度的 |
| possession | *n.* | 佔有，擁有 |
| the beloved | | 愛人，心愛的人 |

Nothing seemed to fit, yet there were plenty of clues to indicate everything was somehow related. I knew the random probability of so many coincidences was zero. (註6)

似乎沒有一件事情符合，但是有很多的線索顯示這一切多少有些關聯。我知道這許多巧合的隨機或然率是零。

| | | |
|---|---|---|
| clue | *n.* | 線索 |
| indicate | *v.* | 指出，顯示 |
| random | *a.* | 隨機的，隨意的 |
| coincidence | *n.* | 巧合；相符 |

**瀏覽全句→查閱單字→細思句意→了解句意（練習翻譯）**

這種練習純屬基本功，需要些許耐性；任何片紙隻字，信手取來，隨時都可作練習。每天讀上幾句英文，不會佔太多時間，養成習慣，大概三個月之後，就可擺脫「文盲」的狀態，邁入「**第二層次的閱讀**」了。

## ● 第二層次的閱讀—— Inspectional Reading 檢驗閱讀

**What is the paragraph about?**

**What are its parts?**

這個段落如何？談到哪些？

　　這是進入「**第二層次的閱讀**」的人，自然會提出的問題。第二層次閱讀的取材，可任意抓取報章雜誌、英文小說的片段——至少五、六句。雖只是斷簡殘篇，但五花八門的題材，卻可拓廣語彙範圍，在三個月之內，即可建立粗淺的閱讀能力。這時，不妨按下列步驟練習閱讀——

　　**略讀全段落→查閱單字→了解各句句意→串連前後句句意→體會全段落意義或了解意思**

During the ebb, I wrote a line upon the sand,

Committing to it all that is in my soul and mind;

I returned at the tide to read it and to ponder upon it,

I found naught upon the seashore but my ignorance. (註7) *體會意義

退潮時，我在沙灘上畫了一道線，

畫出我心靈與思想中的一切；

漲潮時，我重回沙灘，想要讀它且細思時，

我發現沙灘上除了我的無知之外，空無一物。

| | | |
|---|---|---|
| ebb | *n.* | 退潮，落潮 |
| commit sth. to ~ | | 把…寫下來 |
| tide | *n.* | 潮，潮汐 |
| ponder upon | | 仔細思考… |
| naught | *n.* | 零，落空，無物（＝nought） |
| ignorance | *n.* | 無知 |

　　"We have your tickets and itinerary, Velis," he said. "The office is expecting you in Paris next Monday. You'll spend the night there and go on to Algiers in the morning. I'll have the tickets and papers delivered to your apartment this afternoon, if that's all right? " I told him it was fine. (註8) *了解意思

「Velis，這兒有妳的機票和行程。」他說，「公司希望妳下星期一到巴黎，在那兒過一個晚上，然後早上再到Algiers。下午我會把機票和文件送到妳住處，這樣好嗎？」我告訴他沒問題。

| itinerary | *n.* | 行程，旅行計畫 |
|-----------|------|----------------|
| deliver | *v.* | 傳送，寄送 |

Langdon reeled momentarily, lost in her eyes. "When?" He paused, curious if she had any idea how much he had been wondering the same thing. "Well, actually, next month I'm lecturing at a conference in Florence. I'll be there a week without much to do." (註9) *了解意思

Langdon 迷惑了片刻，迷失在她的眼神中。「什麼時候？」他停了一下，很好奇她是否知道他一直對這件事有相當的疑惑。「哦，事實上，我下個月要到 Florence 的一場會議中發表演說。我會在那兒待上一個星期，沒啥事可做。」

| reel | *v.* | 迷惑，搖晃地走 |
|------|------|----------------|
| momentarily | *adv.* | 片刻地，短暫地 |

This elicited a hearty round of laughs. Langdon considered offering an etymological sidebar about the word hermaphrodite and its ties to Hermes and Aphrodite, but something told him it would be lost on this crowd. (註10) *了解意思

這引起了一陣哄堂大笑，Langdon 考慮要提出一個有關 hermaphrodite（雌雄同體）這個字的字源解說，以及和 Hermes（眾神的使者）與 Aphrodite（愛神）的關係。但是，某些事情讓他知道這些人是聽不懂的。

◆hermaphrodite（雌雄同體）→ *herm,* Hermes（眾神的使者，男性）+ *aphrodite,* Aphrodite（愛神，女性）

| elicit | *v.* | 引起（反應） |
|--------|------|--------------|
| round of | | 一陣，一輪 |
| hearty laugh | | 開懷大笑 |
| etymological | *a.* | 字(詞)源學的 |
| sidebar | *n.* | 附屬說明 |
| hermaphrodite | *n.* | 雌雄同體 |

| | |
|---|---|
| be lost on ~ | 對…不起作用 |
| crowd | **n.** 一群人，群眾 |

If this discovery is confirmed, it will surely be one of the most stunning insights into our universe that science has ever uncovered. Its implications are as far-reaching and awe-inspiring as can be imagined. Even as it promises answers to some of our oldest questions, it poses still others even more fundamental. (註11) *了解意思

如果這項發現被證實了，想必它會是一直以來科學所揭開的宇宙最驚人的深入了解事物之一。我們能夠想像得到：它的影響會是深遠而令人敬畏的。甚至，它有可能讓我們部份古老的疑問得到解答，它還會衍生其他更基本的待解的疑問。

| | | |
|---|---|---|
| stunning | **a.** | 驚人的 |
| insight | **n.** | 深入了解，洞悉 |
| implication(s) | **n.** | 可能的影響 |
| far-reaching | **a.** | 深遠的 |
| awe-inspiring | **a.** | 令人敬畏的 |
| pose | **v.** | 造成，導致 |
| fundamental | **a.** | 基本的 |

My soul preached to me and said, "Do not be delighted because of praise, and do not be distressed because of blame."

Ere my soul counseled me, I doubted the worth of my work.

Now I realize that the trees blossom in Spring and bear fruit in Summer without seeking praise; and they drop their leaves in Autumn and become naked in Winter without fearing blame. (註12) *體會意義

我的心靈勸告我：「勿因讚美而沾沾自喜，勿因受責而苦惱憂心。」

在我的心靈忠告我之前，我懷疑我工作的價值。

現在我領悟：樹木在春天開花、夏天結果，不求讚美；而在秋天落葉、冬天盡枯，不懼譴責。

| | | |
|---|---|---|
| delighted | **a.** | 高興的 |
| distressed | **a.** | 苦惱的，憂慮的 |

## ● 第三層次的閱讀── Analytical Reading 分析閱讀

**What is the information about?**

**What does it mean?**

這資料（訊）敘述什麼？有什麼含意？

如果您開始閱讀整篇文章，或較長的段落，而不感到絲毫厭倦。那麼，這表示你已進入「**第三層次的閱讀**」了。在閱讀的過程中，儘可能把握以下的原則：

1. When reading a difficult essay for the first time, read it through without ever stopping to think about the things that you do not understand immediately.
2. Know what kind of essay you are reading and list or outline the major parts of the essay.
3. State briefly the unity of the whole essay and express the problem(s) the author is trying to solve.

同時，除了瞭解文章表面的意思外，也要學習掌握正確的字義，深入了解作者的「情」、作者的「意」。下面幾篇（段）文章，就請讀者閱讀一下吧！

I'll admit there are very deep parts of the ocean floor that oceanographers call dead zones. We don't really understand them, but they are areas in which the currents and food sources are such that almost nothing lives there. Just a few species of bottom-dwelling scavengers. So from that standpoint, I suppose a single-species fossil is not entirely out of the question. (註13)

我承認有非常深的海床地區，海洋學家稱之為死亡地帶。我們並不真正了解它們，但它們是潮流和食物來源少到幾乎沒有生物活在那兒的區域，只存活著少數棲息於海底的吃食腐肉的物種。所以從這個角度來看，我猜測有單一物種的化石，不是完全不可能的。

| oceanographer | *n.* 海洋學家 |
| bottom-dwelling | *a.* 棲息於底部的 |

| | | |
|---|---|---|
| scavenger | *n.* | 食腐肉的動物 |
| standpoint | *n.* | 觀點，角度 |
| single-species | *n.* | 單一物種 |
| fossil | *n.* | 化石 |
| out of the question | | 絕對不可能 |

Like a meteorite striking the dark side of the moon, the rock crashed into a vast plain of mud on the ocean floor, kicking up a cloud of silt. As the dust settled, one of the ocean's thousands of unknown species swam over to inspect the odd newcomer. Unimpressed, the creature moved on. (註14)

就像隕石撞擊月球的陰暗面一樣，巨石墜落在海床廣大平坦的泥地，掀起一團淤泥。等塵埃落定，海洋中數千種不知名的物種之一，游過來檢視這個古怪的新來者。這生物對它一點也不感興趣，仍繼續前進。

| | | |
|---|---|---|
| meteorite | *n.* | 隕石 |
| kick up | | 揚起，掀起 |
| a cloud of ~ | | 一團… |
| silt | *n.* | 淤泥，(沉積的)泥沙 |
| unimpressed | *a.* | 無深刻印象的；認為不重要的 |

Buffett had talked many times before about mistakes. But when he spoke, as he often did, of his mistakes of omission, he never ventured beyond business mistakes. The errors of omission in his personal life — inattention, neglect, missed chances — were always there, the side effects of intensity; but they were shadow presences visible only to those who knew him well. He spoke of them only in private, if at all. (註15)

Buffett以前曾多次提到他的錯誤，但是他說到他的無心之過時（他常說），卻從不敢提商場失算以外的錯誤。他個人生活中的無心錯誤──漫不經心、疏忽、錯失機會──經常發生，這是緊張的副作用；但這些錯誤彷如影子的存在，只有熟識他的人才看得見。如此，他也只在私下提到這些錯誤。

| | | |
|---|---|---|
| omission | *n.* | 疏忽，遺漏 |
| venture | *v.* | 敢說，大膽表示 |
| inattention | *n.* | 漫不經心，疏忽 |

| | | |
|---|---|---|
| neglect | *n.* | 忽略，疏忽 |
| side effect | | 副作用 |
| intensity | *n.* | 強烈程度 |
| shadow | *n.* | 影子，陰影 |
| visible | *a.* | 看得見的 |

"Molecule for molecule, methane's heat-trapping power in the atmosphere is twenty-one times stronger than carbon dioxide, the most abundant greenhouse gas," reported *Science World* (January 21, 2002). "With 1.3 billion cows belching almost constantly around the world (100 million in the United States alone), it's no surprise that methane released by livestock is one of the chief global sources of the gas, according to the U.S. Environmental Protection Agency … 'It's part of their normal digestion process,' says Tom Wirth of the EPA. 'When they chew their cud, they regurgitate [spit up] some food to rechew it, and all this gas comes out.' The average cow expels 600 liters of methane a day, climate researchers report." (註16)

「大氣中每分子的沼氣（甲烷）聚熱能量，要比二氧化碳強21倍，是最大量的溫室氣體。」《科學世界》在2002年1月21日如此報導：「據美國環境保護局表示：全世界有13億頭牛幾乎不斷地在打嗝（光是美國就有一億頭牛），而牲畜釋放的甲烷是全球溫室氣體的主要來源之一，這沒什麼奇怪的…環境保護局　Tom Wirth表示：『那是牠們的正常消化過程；當牠們反芻時，吐出一些食物，再咀嚼它，同時排出所有氣體。』氣候研究人員說：一頭牛平均每天排放600公升的甲烷

| | | |
|---|---|---|
| molecule | *n.* | 分子 |
| methane | *n.* | 沼氣，甲烷 |
| heat-trapping | *n.* | 聚熱的 |
| carbon dioxide | | 二氧化碳 |
| abundant | *a.* | 大量的，充裕的 |
| belching | *n.* | 打嗝 |
| livestock | *n.* | 牲畜 |
| digestion | *n.* | 消化 |
| cud | *n.* | 反芻的食物 |
| regurgitate | *v.* | 反芻 |
| liter | *n.* | 公升 |

## ● 第四層次的閱讀── Syntopical Reading 綜合主題閱讀

第四層次的閱讀，也可說是 Comparative Reading（比較閱讀）。能堅持到這種閱讀層次的人，其耐性和毅力，實在令人感佩。因為進行到此一地步，就必須拿同一作者的不同作品，或不同作者同一題材的文章，作分析、比較，甚至寫下心得、評論。好比說，您要是看了 Dan Brown 的 The Da Vinci Code，再看他的其他作品：Angles and Demons、Deception Point，或者更早寫的 Digital Fortress。不要只是看懂就算了，不妨嘗試著比較一下這些 Science Fiction 的風格和 Dan Brown 異想天開的創意。又例如，Mark Twain（原名 Clemens, Samuel Langhorone）的作品有 Adventures of Huckleberry Finn、The Adventure of Tom Sawyer、The Prince And The Pauper、Tom Sawyer Abroad、Tom Sawyer Detective、The Mysterious Stranger 等。看過之後，分析比較之下，您就知道 Mark Twain 在美國文學史上的崇高地位，以及他何以被稱作 humorist（幽默作家）！再說如果您看完前美國副總統 Core 的 An Inconvenient Truth，再看完 Thomas L. Friedman 撰寫的 Hot, Flat, And Growded 和 Gale E. Christianson 著的 Greenhouse—The 200-year Story of Global Warming，以及 Alan Weisman 寫的 The World Without Us，對地球和人類的明天，您作何感想、有何感慨呢？

總之，「第四層次的閱讀」是需要大量閱讀，也需要作深入的思索和探討。但是「有為者亦若是」，如果您能養成閱讀的習慣，持之以恆，「熟讀唐詩三百首，不能作詩也能吟」，您的英文寫作能力也會跟著大幅提升呢！

【註】

(註1、15)　摘錄自 Alice Schroeder 著 *The Snowball* 第55章 The Last Kay Party
(註2、13)　摘錄自 Dan Brown 著 *Deception Point* 第82章
(註3、16)　摘錄自 Thomas L. Friedman 著 *Hot, Flat, And Crowded* 第二章 Today's Date: 1 E.C.E
(註4、6、8)　摘錄自 Katherine Neville 著 *The Eight* 的 The Knight's Wheel
(註5、7、12)　摘錄自 Gibran Kahlil Gibran 著 *The Wisdom Of Gibran*
(註9、10)　摘錄自 Dan Brown 著 *The Da Vinci Code* 第105、26章
(註11)　摘錄自1997年8月7日發現 ALH84001 火星隕石時，美國總統 Bill Clinton 在記者會中的致詞。
(註14)　摘錄自 Dan Brown 著 *Deception Point* 的 Epiloque

# Full-Length
# New TOEIC Practice Test

## 完整200題仿真測驗題

## LISTENING TEST

In the Listening test, you will be asked to demonstrate how well you understand spoken English. The entire Listening test will last approximately 45 minutes. There are four parts, and directions are given for each part. You must mark your answers on the separate answer sheet. Do not write your answers in the test book.

### Part 1

**Directions:** For each question in this part, you will hear four statements about a picture in your test book. When you hear the statements, you must select the one statement that best describes what you see in the picture. Then find the number of the question on your answer sheet and mark your answer. The statements will not be printed in your test book and will be spoken only one time.

Sample Answer

Statement (C), "They're standing near the table," is the best description of the picture, so you should select answer (C) and mark it on your answer sheet.

**1.**

**2.**

GO ON TO THE NEXT PAGE.

新｜版｜多｜益｜測｜驗｜攻｜略

**3.**

**4.**

**5.**

**6.**

**GO ON TO THE NEXT PAGE.**

新｜版｜多｜益｜測｜驗｜攻｜略

**7.**

**8.**

**9.**

**9.**

**10.**

**GO ON TO THE NEXT PAGE.**

新 | 版 | 多 | 益 | 測 | 驗 | 攻 | 略

## Part 2

**Directions:** You will hear a question or statement and three responses spoken in English. They will be spoken only one time and will not be printed in your test book. Select the best response to the question or statement and mark the letter (A), (B), or (C) on your answer sheet. For example,

You will hear :      Where is the meeting room?
You will also hear :   (A) To meet the new director.
                  (B) It's the first room on the right.
                  (C) Yes, at two o'clock.

 Sample Answer

The best response to the question "Where is the meeting room?" is choice (B), "It's the first room on the right," so (B) is the correct answer. You should mark answer (B) on your answer sheet.

**11.** Mark your answer on your answer sheet.
**12.** Mark your answer on your answer sheet.
**13.** Mark your answer on your answer sheet.
**14.** Mark your answer on your answer sheet.
**15.** Mark your answer on your answer sheet.
**16.** Mark your answer on your answer sheet.
**17.** Mark your answer on your answer sheet.
**18.** Mark your answer on your answer sheet.
**19.** Mark your answer on your answer sheet.
**20.** Mark your answer on your answer sheet.
**21.** Mark your answer on your answer sheet.
**22.** Mark your answer on your answer sheet.
**23.** Mark your answer on your answer sheet.
**24.** Mark your answer on your answer sheet.
**25.** Mark your answer on your answer sheet.

**26.** Mark your answer on your answer sheet.
**27.** Mark your answer on your answer sheet.
**28.** Mark your answer on your answer sheet.
**29.** Mark your answer on your answer sheet.
**30.** Mark your answer on your answer sheet.
**31.** Mark your answer on your answer sheet.
**32.** Mark your answer on your answer sheet.
**33.** Mark your answer on your answer sheet.
**34.** Mark your answer on your answer sheet.
**35.** Mark your answer on your answer sheet.
**36.** Mark your answer on your answer sheet.
**37.** Mark your answer on your answer sheet.
**38.** Mark your answer on your answer sheet.
**39.** Mark your answer on your answer sheet.
**40.** Mark your answer on your answer sheet.

## Part 3

**Directions:** You will hear some conversations between two people. You will be asked to answer three questions about what the speakers say in each conversation. Select the best response to each question and mark the letter (A), (B), (C), or (D) on your answer sheet. The conversations will be spoken only one time and will not be printed in your test book.

**41.** What did the man do?
(A) Making 10 copies of the proposal
(B) Producing diagrams
(C) Setting up the conference room
(D) Visiting Mr. Sanders

**42.** What are the speakers preparing for?
(A) A press conference
(B) A meeting presentation
(C) A wedding proposal
(D) A new association

**43.** Where will the meeting most likely take place?
(A) At a local bar
(B) In a conference room
(C) At a convention center
(D) On a computer

**44.** What is the purpose of the call?
(A) To inquire about internet access
(B) To apply for a credit card
(C) To register for a membership
(D) To give personal information

**45.** Why did the woman ask for the man's personal information?
(A) To input them into a database
(B) To confirm his identity
(C) To update his billing address
(D) To renew his subscription

**46.** What problem did the man have?
(A) His phone connection is down.
(B) His credit card was stolen.
(C) He can't go online.
(D) He wants to cancel his service.

**GO ON TO THE NEXT PAGE.**

新 | 版 | 多 | 益 | 測 | 驗 | 攻 | 略

**47.** Why did the woman call?
  (A) To book a room
  (B) To cancel a reservation
  (C) To request for a smaller room
  (D) To change a check-in date

**48.** When will the woman arrive?
  (A) On the nineteenth
  (B) On the twentieth
  (C) On the twenty third
  (D) On the twenty fifth

**49.** What is the woman likely to do?
  (A) Keep the same room
  (B) Move to a suite
  (C) Get a single room
  (D) Cancel her reservation

**50.** What are the speakers waiting for?
  (A) A taxicab
  (B) A shuttle bus
  (C) An express train
  (D) A rental car

**51.** What is the problem?
  (A) The shuttle is late.
  (B) There is no taxi available.
  (C) They have the wrong schedule.
  (D) They lost the hotel address.

**52.** What does the man suggest?
  (A) Ask for the taxi rate
  (B) Wait for their ride
  (C) Get the hotel address
  (D) Visit a car rental service

**53.** Who installed the projector screen?
  (A) Sharon
  (B) Kevin
  (C) The director
  (D) A technician

**54.** What will the woman do tomorrow?
  (A) Speak with the director
  (B) Install the new screens
  (C) Contact the technician
  (D) Change the lighting

**55.** How does the director feel about the new screens?
  (A) Satisfied
  (B) Disappointed
  (C) Excited
  (D) Unhappy

**56.** Who isn't going to watch the film?
- (A) Michael
- (B) Vanessa
- (C) Tiffany
- (D) Daisy

**57.** How do critics feel about the movie?
- (A) Generally positive.
- (B) They hated it.
- (C) It was a relief.
- (D) Quite negative.

**58.** What will Vanessa do?
- (A) Read the reviews
- (B) See the film
- (C) Wait for the video
- (D) Watch another movie

**59.** Where is this conversation taking place?
- (A) Over the phone
- (B) At a meeting
- (C) On a website
- (D) In a store

**60.** When will the shipment arrive?
- (A) Tomorrow morning
- (B) Tomorrow evening
- (C) On the fifth of May
- (D) Next year

**61.** Why did the man apologize?
- (A) There was an error on the disclaimer.
- (B) The shipment will be late.
- (C) The batteries are not working.
- (D) The offer is no longer valid.

**62.** What happened to the woman?
- (A) She was fired.
- (B) She was criticized.
- (C) She got a promotion.
- (D) She missed her meeting.

**63.** What is probably the woman's job position?
- (A) A board member
- (B) An economist
- (C) A team leader
- (D) An observer

**64.** How does the woman feel about Mr. Cooper's evaluation?
- (A) Groundless
- (B) Constructive
- (C) Meaningless
- (D) Useless

**GO ON TO THE NEXT PAGE.**

新｜版｜多｜益｜測｜驗｜攻｜略

**65.** What does Michael plan to do?
(A) Postpone a report
(B) Speak with bookkeepers
(C) Call the accounting director
(D) Visit the apartment units

**66.** What are the speakers mainly talking about?
(A) An accounting director
(B) A profit estimate
(C) Apartment units
(D) An audit report

**67.** When is the deadline for the audit?
(A) Today
(B) Tuesday
(C) Friday
(D) Saturday

**68.** What do the speakers most likely do?
(A) Electronic engineers
(B) Stock analysts
(C) Accountants
(D) Production managers

**69.** What does the man suggest the woman do?
(A) Fix the technical glitches
(B) Give him some change
(C) Take another look at her analysis
(D) Speak to an accountant

**70.** What type of business does KCR probably do?
(A) Bank accounts
(B) Stock exchange
(C) Electronic products
(D) Technical advice

**160.** Which topic does the notice concern?

(A) Anti-contamination and eco-friendliness

(B) Protecting consumer rights

(C) Tour guide

(D) Rubbish dump

**161.** How may pets do fish any harm?

(A) Disordering their laying eggs

(B) Eating them up

(C) Keeping them on leash

(D) Biting them to death

**162.** What can be inferred from the passage?

(A) We can freely use sources of drinking water.

(B) Exploring a particular field is good for human beings.

(C) Toilet facilities are provided for hikers.

(D) Even decomposable products will be harmful to the environment.

新｜版｜多｜益｜測｜驗｜攻｜略

## *LEATHER CARE    DOs" and    DON'Ts"*

With proper care, your leather garments should last a very long time. Keep in mind that regular use enhances the appearance of your leather wear. So go ahead, wear your leather garments often.

### ●**Storage**
1. Keep in a well-ventilated, cool, dry place.
2. Store your leather wear on a well-shaped wooden, plastic or padded hanger.

### ●**Care**
1. Apply a high quality leather lotion on a soft cloth to clean and moisturize your finished leather. Hang dry.
2. If your leather becomes wet, allow it to dry naturally at room temperature. When dry, apply a leather protector.
3. Liquid stains should be gently cleaned with a damp cloth. If stains linger, clean with a leather cleaning solution.

### ● **"Don'ts"**
1. Don't put your leather wear in the dryer.
2. Don't store leather in direct sunlight or hot places such as attics or parked cars.
3. Don't use plastic bags for storing leather. This can cause excessive dryness.

**163**. How should wet leather be treated?
(A) It should be hung outside.
(B) It should be dried in a dryer.
(C) It should be patted dry with a towel.
(D) It should be dried indoors.

**164.** When should a leather cleaning solution be used?
(A) Whenever a leather garment is stored
(B) When a dry cloth is ineffective
(C) When there is difficulty removing a stain
(D) Whenever a leather garment is stained

**165.** How can a leather garment's appearance be enhanced?
(A) By avoiding the use of hangers
(B) By wearing it frequently
(C) By storing it at room temperature
(D) By storing it in a plastic bag

**Questions 166-169** refer to the following e-mail.

| To: | bioservice@biochemhealth.com |
|---|---|
| From: | Valentina Erny < vaerny@twinpeaks.com > |
| Subject: | Return Shipment & Demand Reimbursement |
| Date: | May 21, 2010 |

Dear Sir / Ma'am,

I am writing this e-mail to you with regard to an order I placed 20 DAYS ago on May 1 via your on-line shopping Website. The order number was KM080401-678.

The order that I placed included the following products.
1. Titan Complex Vitamin, 3 bottles (100-pill size)
2. GraceEve Chlorella, 2 boxes (200-tablet size)
3. Hercules Herb Extract, 3 boxes (150-tablet size)

The total for the order was $195.95, including tax and priority shipping.

I received my order this morning 13 DAYS later than had been promised to me even though I paid an extra $8.00 for a holiday rush order. However, this was not the only problem. Upon opening the package, I noticed that there was only one box of chlorella tablets that I ordered two. The other one was not to be found anywhere. Furthermore, the cap on one of the Vitamin bottles had been completely torn off.

Because of this, I am returning the shipment to you. I hope that you will ship a new replacement order by express, as well as refund the cost of the priority shipping fee that I paid. I would also hope that you would reimburse the shipping fee for the return shipment that I am sending back to you. Please check your records, and send the replacement to me asap.

Thank you for your help,
Valentina Erny

**166.** What was one of the problems with the order?

(A) The pills were poor in quality.

(B) One of the items was damaged.

(C) The vitamin was missing.

(D) She was charged too much.

**167.** When did the writer expect her order to arrive?

(A) May 21

(B) May 8

(C) May 1

(D) May 13

**168.** What did the writer ask for?

(A) A new order

(B) A partial refund

(C) A full refund

(D) A new product

**169.** How much was the priority shipping fee?

(A) $195.95 including tax

(B) $195.95

(C) $8.00

(D) $2.00

Bellboys expect a $1 minimum per bag; in luxury hotels $2 each or $5 for several bags. No tip is necessary for the desk clerk, elevator operator or concierge but a $1 minimum is normal for the doorman on arrival, more if he provides special service. A $1 tip to the doorman for calling a taxi is standard. The roommaid should get $2 per night left in an envelope marked 'For the maid'.

**170.** Who is a tip UNnecessary for?

(A) The doorman

(B) The roommaid

(C) The desk clerk

(D) The bellboy

**171.** What is this passage about?

(A) A tip on tips

(B) A hotel ad.

(C) A want ad.

(D) A precaution

**172.** How much should you give the cleaner per night as a tip?

(A) $1

(B) $5

(C) $2

(D) $3

# Phone Banking Directions

A | Choose from the following options:

1. Bank Service Information 　　4. Address / Account Changes
2. Balance / Transaction Inquiries 　5. Current Exchange and Interest Rates
3. To report a lost or stolen card 　6. Customer Service

B | Enter your 16-digit account number

C | Enter your secret code

※ You can press "0" at any time to inquire with a Customer Service representative.

1. Account balances are of the current business day or as of the previous business day if calling between 4 p.m. and 9 a.m. weekdays.
2. Account balances are of the previous business day if calling on weekends and / or bank holidays.
3. Transactions done by phone after 4 p.m. will not be credited until the next business day.
4. Transactions such as inter-account transfers done by phone will not be credited until the next business day.
5. Address / Account changes done by phone are effective as of the following business day regardless of time.

**173.** What kind of banking service is being offered?
(A) After service
(B) Audiovisual service
(C) Automated service
(D) Door-to-door service

**174.** When will an address change done on Friday at 2 p.m. be effective?
(A) Next Monday
(B) After 4 p.m.
(C) At the moment
(D) The current business day

**175.** When will a transaction done by phone at 5 p.m. be credited?
(A) On the current business day
(B) On the previous business day
(C) On the next business day
(D) On the bank holiday

**176.** What would you press for your account balance?
(A) 6
(B) 5
(C) 3
(D) 2

**Questions 177-180** refer to the following message.

Anyone contemplating taking the circuit trip should come to the park well prepared and well equipped. While it is true that many canoeists with only limited experience have successfully completed the circuit, good physical condition and good equipment are essential. Since Cu Cu Lake National Park is essentially an undeveloped wilderness, users of the waterway can expect to experience conditions similar to the hazards and hardships of pioneer travel. The circuit can be completed in six to seven days but those wishing to fish and relax may prefer to stay longer. It is possible to be stormbound for several days.

**177.** How long will the trip take?
(A) Half a month
(B) Nearly a week
(C) More than two months
(D) A couple of days

**178.** What should the tourists be careful of in this area?
(A) Wild animals
(B) Abandoned wells
(C) Dangerous waterway
(D) Canoeist

**179.** What is the park described as?
(A) An abandoned place
(B) An uncultivated area
(C) A flowery field
(D) A badlands

**180.** How is the waterway in the park described?
(A) It is unsafe.
(B) It is tranquil.
(C) It is bumpy.
(D) It is stormy.

新 | 版 | 多 | 益 | 測 | 驗 | 攻 | 略

**Questions 181-185** refer to the following e-mails.

| To: | Simon <simon@globalmate.com> |
|-----|-------------------------------|
| From: | Akio Nakamura <akionakamura@kchpr.com> |
| Subject: | How's it going? |

Simon,

How's it going? Haven't heard from you for quite some time.

I've been back in Tokyo for four months now. So far life's been fine to me. I am working for KCH Public Relations Company as a creative researcher. This company is quite young, but the officemates are really energetic. You've got to be here to feel their dynamic spirit. All people and things move around me at such a pace that it is never as dull as ditchwater. My job is quite heavy, but I must say I've learnt a lot from it and have made lots of good contacts.

I have to keep myself updated all the time, because living and working in Toyko is truly international. Toyko is a very cosmopolitan city and it's really a great place to train up newcomers.

Recently I got myself involved in a ninety-thousand-dollar project promoting a portfolio. Sure there were sleepless nights when planning for it. Yet I'm more excited and happier than I used to be. And how about you? How about your job?

Remember, all work and no play will make your life deadly boring!

Best Wishes,
Akio

| To: | Akio Nakamura <akionakamura@kchpr.com> |
| From: | Simon <simon@globalmate.com> |
| Subject: | About my job. |

Akio,

Thank you for your e-mail yesterday. It is true that I have not written to you for a couple of months. This e-mail should put you in the picture about my job.

As I said in the last e-mail, the launch of our automatic color press in China last fall was rather low-key. Competitors' machines are manufactured locally and marketed aggressively at irresistible prices. Up to now, imported machines like ours have been subject to 30% duty and 20% sales tax. The only weakness of our machine has been its cost. The high price of the machine prohibits customers from buying it. And one of the main disadvantages for us has been our inability to find a highly motivated agent to promote our products. So we find it hard to gain market share here. Yet the intensively competitive pressure of the trade is favorable.

An article which appeared in last week's *Press Technology Weekly* praised the automatic color press highly. That sounds good for us. All for now. I hope you have a great success in your field.

Keep in touch.
Simon

181. Which is NOT addressed in these
    e-mails?
    (A) Trade pressure
    (B) Printing press
    (C) International city
    (D) On-the-job training

182. What is Simon's e-mail mainly
    about?
    (A) Overtime work
    (B) Intense trade competition
    (C) How to promote his company's
        products
    (D) Promoting a portfolio

183. In Akio's e-mail, the idiom "dull as
    ditchwater" in paragraph 2, line 6, is
    closest in meaning to _____.
    (A) monotonous
    (B) colourful
    (C) adventurous
    (D) censorious

184. How is the duty and tax of the
    imported press described?
    (A) It is tax-deductible.
    (B) It is tax-exempt.
    (C) It is a heavy burden.
    (D) It is duty-free.

185. According to the e-mail, which is
    the detriment to the imported color
    press?
    (A) Irresistible price
    (B) No aggressive agent
    (C) Less advertising
    (D) No customer service

**Questions 186-190** refer to the following reports.

Japanese adults by the hundreds of thousands — young and old — are going to classrooms across the islands to pursue new goals and fulfillment in life. Adults are now the fastest-growing segment of Japanese education and are likely to remain so for years to come. In 2007, about 5 million adult Japanese were attending school or college part time. Today the total comes to almost 9 million enrolled in instructional programs at college campuses, community centers, cram schools and medical centers. Classes adults are taking courses including sculpturing, painting, yoga relaxation, birdwatching, classical-music appreciation, photography, dancing and weaving. What educators are discovering is that many adults come back to school not just to fill time, or learn a job or hobby, but to enlarge their understanding of themselves, their lives and their relationship to the world around them.

Specialists find that 3 out of every 7 peole in our country are relaxing — away from paid jobs — in painting, performing music, weaving, wood carving and other hobbies. There are also estimates that about 10 percent of homes have ardent amateur gardeners who take care of greenery from house plants to large vegetable gardens. Two percent collect stamps and about 30 thousand are amateur photographers. An estimated 80 thousand regularly participate in organized dance courses.

One of the main reasons for the prosperity, observers say, is that our contemporary countrymen feel a deep need to escape the routine of their jobs. In leisure time, they turn to hobbies for a kind of individual self-expression and relaxation. For example, social psychologists say, most people choose hobbies in which at least a small amount of physical labor is involved. They also choose hobbies which provide immediate evidence of results. Such activities often are in contrast to their jobs, which involve many other people, no single one of whom can point to a product and say, "That was made entirely by me." Director Simon Liu of the Social Bureau says, "It's not just using your hands to make things. It's the sense of personal achievement that comes from doing a job from beginning to end."

**186.** What is implied in these reports?
(A) Hobbies are not participatory.
(B) Many adults have the urge to know and continue to grow.
(C) Many adults come back to school just for fun.
(D) Japanese want just to watch those talented artists.

**187.** According to these passages, which topic is appropriate?
(A) Learning has more meaning than it has purpose
(B) The warm feeling of achievement
(C) Self-renewal takes new directions in hobbies, back-to-school
(D) Hobbies are good for health

**188.** Which of the following is NOT discussed in these passages?
(A) Gardening
(B) Sculpturing
(C) Aerobics
(D) Antique collecting

**189.** What is the main explanation of why adults pick up new hobbies?
(A) Adults want to expand their interests.
(B) Hobbies have fulfilled adults' childhood dream.
(C) Adults intend to kill time.
(D) Hobbies often serve to focus self-awareness.

**190.** What is NOT mentioned as a reason for people choosing hobbies?
(A) People don't like unchangeable work.
(B) People like to relax themselves in leisure time.
(C) People often take part in activities which involve many other people.
(D) People don't like to make things entirely by themselves.

**Questions 191-195** refer to the following advertisement and e-mail.

# *Help Wanted*
## People with Web page design abilities wanted!

If you already have a job but want to earn more money in
your spare time, please tell us about your Web abilities.
We are only interested in your ability to create the product.
Now, let your creativity be a key to extra money!
If this appeals to you, please contact HR A.S.A.P. by email at
webdesign@comsat.com

| To: | HR  <webdesign@comsat.com> |
|------|-----|
| From: | Marina Cott <marinac@duredu.com> |
| Subject: | Apply for a job |

To whom it may concern,

I'm writing to you in reference to the advertisement you have placed in the April 10th edition of the Financial Daily.

As you'll note in the enclosed résumé, I have had extensive experience in the field of computers. Since my graduation from UC Berkerly, I have had the chance to work with top firms in the computer industry. With my knowledge and expertise, I feel that I can be an asset to your company. I hope that you'll give me the opportunity to show this.

Please feel free to contact me at any time. I look forward to hearing from you.

Sincerely yours,
**Marina Cott**

**191.** What kind of the email is it?

(A) A cover letter

(B) An e-mail to the columnist

(C) An e-mail of recommendation

(D) A résumé

**192.** What kind of person could not do this job?

(A) A person who only has weekends off

(B) A person with no free time

(C) An engineer

(D) A college student

**193.** Why was this e-mail written?

(A) To reply to an ad

(B) To apply for a job

(C) To keep in touch with someone

(D) To sell computers

**194.** Which characteristic would be best for this job?

(A) Sense of humor

(B) Diligence

(C) Loyalty

(D) Inventiveness

**195.** Which of the following is essential to this job?

(A) Ability to create Web pages

(B) Experience at a Web company

(C) New approach to management

(D) Working hours

## ☰☰☰ **Financialweekly**

Date: March 31, 2010

Dear Past Subscriber,

As our valued reader, we are happy to bring you an exceptional offer from Financialweekly. We are offering an exclusive and irresistible rate to past readers!

The global finance is reeling under rapid change in economic situations of most areas. Keeping up with financial events is difficult enough, not to mention understanding their full effects and how they will unfold. Financialweekly can help you understand!

With Financialweekly you'll get the key whys and wherefores on every report and you'll be among the first to know about significant financial events, ahead of any mass media.

You can have the benefit of this very special renewal subscription offer and have Financialweekly delivered to your home or office, at a privileged price of up to 60% less than what you would pay at the newsstand or bookstore.

We urge you to send back the order form below today and join the worldwide team of well-informed Financialweekly readers again. You'll appreciate Financialweekly's professional and forward-looking perspective at the beginning of the 21st century.

Yours sincerely,

*Thomas Guoa*

Thomas Guao
General Manager
Asia Edition

P.S.   # If you're ever dissatisfied, for any reason, you may cancel your subscription and receive a full refund on all unmailed issues. No questions asked.

A 'Best Buy' 78-issue subscription saves you NT$7,488 and at 52-issue subscription saves you NT$4,576. Please remember to return your order form before July 31, 2010.

Financialweekly's cover price is NT$160. For enquiries, please call (8862)2389-9808, fax (8862)2389-9167 or email us at: best.service@financialweekly.com.tw

# Financialweekly Special Subscription Order Form

**SAVE UP TO 60%**

Special subscription offer for Past Subscriber

Please tick:
- ☑ 18 months ( 78 issues ) at NT$ 64 per copy for a tatal of NT$4,922
- ☐ 12 months ( 52 issues ) at NT$ 72 per copy for a tatal of NT$3,744

Valid until: July 31, 2010  (DM0708TW)

**PAYMENT METHOD:**

☐ Bill me later

☑ Please charge to Credit Card
( Indicate which )

- ☐ Visa  ☑ MasterCard
- ☐ JCBCard  ☐ Amex

Card Expiry Date
Month / Year
03 2013

Card Number
5468-4700-0262-8400

Your Signature
Amy Kao

Telephone No.
(8862)23899145

E-mail Address
amykao@toeicmate.com.tw

45433727          DM0708TW

**MS  AMY KAO**

**P O  BOX 33-200 TAIPEI**
**TAIPEI CITY 10099, TAIWAN, ROC**

Once subcribed, you may be contacted for the purposes of market reserch and / or direct marketing. Please tick here if you prefer not to be contacted for these purposes by:

☑ Financialweekly International
☑ Other companies

## MONEY BACK GUARANTEE

If you're ever  dissatisified, for any reason, you may cancel your subscription and receive a full refund on unmailed issues. No questions asked.

**196.** What is the purpose of the letter?
- (A) To do a market research
- (B) To push a marketing campaign
- (C) To contact the reader to renew his subscription
- (D) To offer the reader a special gift

**197.** By what date should renewal subscribers respond to Financialweekly?
- (A) March 31
- (B) July 31
- (C) payday
- (D) anytime

**198.** What did Thomas Guoa send with his letter?
- (A) Subscription order form
- (B) Price list
- (C) "Best Buy" offer
- (D) Full refund

**199.** How much can you save when you place a one-year subscription order?
- (A) NT$4,922
- (B) NT$3,744
- (C) NT$4,576
- (D) NT$7,488

**200.** In the letter, the phrase "whys and wherefores" in paragraph 3, line 1, is closest in meaning to _____.
- (A) the reasons and explanations
- (B) cause and effect
- (C) research and development
- (D) perfection and defect

■ Stop! This is the end of the test. If you finish before time is called, you may go back to Parts 5, 6, and 7 and check your work.

# Full-Length
# New TOEIC
# Practice Test 翻譯與解答

▶TRACKS 1-8

# Part 1 Photographs

## 「照片描述」的特點與對策

### 題型說明

　　在這個部份共有 10 題，每題會有一張照片，你會聽到針對每張照片所做的四段描述，每題只會播放一次，播放內容不會印在試題本上，在四個選項之中，請選擇將照片描述的最完整的句子。

### 基本對策

**1** 每題間隔 5 秒，作題時應快速瀏覽照片，利用照片中的線索和情境幫助作答。照片可分為「人、事、地、物」，通常會問「在做什麼」、「什麼職業、身分、表情」、「什麼地點、物件的位置」……。選擇描述最為正確完整的句子作答。

**2** 對答案沒把握時，則適用「刪去法」。先把可以確定不對的選項刪去，再從剩下的選項中 Try your luck. 完全不懂就趕快猜吧！（不倒扣啦！）

**3** 特別注意「多義字」、「同音異義 字」、「渾淆音」等容易誤導判斷的發音，並針對「相關字組」做聯想字彙的練習。

1.

聽力原文 (A) The man is planting the flowers.

(B) The man is resting outside the florist.

(C) The man is sitting in the garden.

(D) The man is arranging a bouquet.

中文翻譯 (A) 男士在種花。

(B) 男士在花店外面休息。

(C) 男士坐在花園裏。

(D) 男士在整理花束。

解　答 **(B)**

註　解

| | | | |
|---|---|---|---|
| plant | v. 種植 | florist | n. 花店，賣花人 |
| arrange | v. 安排，整理 | bouquet | n. 花束 |

**2.**

聽力原文   (A) The waiter is taking their order.

(B) The men are repairing the server.

(C) One of the terminals is not working.

(D) All the computers are occupied.

---

中文翻譯   (A) 服務生在為他們點菜。

(B) 男士正在修理伺服器。

(C) 其中一台電腦故障。

(D) 所有電腦都有人在用。

解　答   **(C)**

註　解

| | | | |
|---|---|---|---|
| take one's order | 幫某人點菜 | server | n. 伺服器，分菜匙 |
| terminal | n. 終端機，終點站 | not working | 故障 |
| occupied | a. 使用中，被佔用 | | |

**3.**

聽力原文 (A) The trolleys are parked along the curb.

(B) Some commuters are boarding the train.

(C) The buses are passing an intersection.

(D) The vans are about to leave the station.

---

中文翻譯 (A) 電車沿著路邊停靠。　　　　　　　　解　答　**(A)**

(B) 一些通勤者在上火車。

(C) 公車正通過一個十字路口。

(D) 小貨車正要駛離車站。

註　解

| | | | |
|---|---|---|---|
| trolley | n. 無軌電車 | park | v. 停放 n. 公園 |
| curb | n. 路邊；邊欄 | commuter | n. 通勤者 |
| board | v. 登上 | intersection | n. 十字路口 |
| van | n. 小貨車，廂型車 | be about to V | 即將，正要 |

4.

聽力原文 (A) The garbageman is collecting trash.
(B) The barrels are attached to the floor.
(C) The waste bins are overloaded with garbage.
(D) The containers are positioned outdoors.

中文翻譯 (A) 清潔人員正在收垃圾。
(B) 桶子固定在地板上。
(C) 垃圾桶內塞滿了垃圾。
(D) 容器裝設在戶外。

解　答 **(D)**

註　解

| | | | |
|---|---|---|---|
| garbageman | v. 垃圾清運人員 | collect | v. 收集 |
| trash | n. 垃圾，廢物 | barrel | n. 大桶，油桶 |
| attach | v. 附著於；連接 | waste bin | 廢紙簍，垃圾桶 |
| overloaded | a. 裝載過多的 | container | n. 容器 |
| position | v. 安置，放在 | | |

**5.**

聽力原文 (A) People are having a discussion.

(B) People are gathering around the seats.

(C) People are facing different dierctions.

(D) People are getting off the transport.

中文翻譯 (A) 這些人在討論事情。

(B) 這些人聚集在座位周遭。

(C) 這些人面對不同方向。

(D) 這些人正在下車。

解　答 **(C)**

註　解

| discussion | n. 討論 | gather | v. 集合，聚集 |
|---|---|---|---|
| face | v. 面向 | direction | n. 方向 |
| get off | 下（交通工具） | transport | n. 交通工具 |

**6.**

聽力原文 (A) Someone is sitting in a yacht.

(B) The ship is being loaded with goods.

(C) The ferry is docked at the shore.

(D) A boat is submerged in the water.

---

中文翻譯 (A) 有個人坐在快艇上。

(B) 船隻正在裝載貨物。

(C) 渡輪停泊在岸邊。

(D) 船隻沉沒在水裡。

解　答 **(A)**

註　解

| | | | |
|---|---|---|---|
| yacht | n. 快艇 | load | v. 裝載 |
| goods | n. 貨物 | ferry | n. 渡輪 |
| dock | v. 停泊 n. 碼頭 | shore | n. 岸邊 |
| submerge | v. 淹沒 | | |

**7.**

聽力原文 (A) An apartment stands above the stairs.

(B) A statue stands behind the courthouse.

(C) The street is lined with statues.

(D) There are trees in front of the structure.

---

中文翻譯 (A) 一幢公寓矗立在階梯上。

(B) 一座雕像矗立在法院後面。

(C) 街道上雕像林列。

(D) 建築物前面有樹叢。

解　答 **(D)**

註　解

| | | | |
|---|---|---|---|
| apartment | n. 公寓 | stairs | n. 階梯 |
| statue | n. 雕像 | courthouse | n. 法院大樓 |
| line | v. 排列，排隊 | structure | n. 建築物 |

**8.**

聽力原文 (A) The man is holding onto a baby stroller.

(B) The child is standing in a puddle of water.

(C) The girl has both her legs in the pond.

(D) They are seated next to water fountain.

---

中文翻譯 (A) 男士抓著一輛嬰兒車。 　　　　　　　　　　　　　　解　答 **(A)**

(B) 小孩子站在水坑裏。

(C) 女孩的雙腳都在水中。

(D) 他們坐在噴泉旁邊。

註　解

| | | | |
|---|---|---|---|
| baby stroller | 嬰兒車 | puddle | n. 水坑 |
| pond | n. 池塘 | fountain | n. 噴泉 |

**9.**

Part

1

聽力原文 (A) The tourists are standing in line on the platfrom.

(B) The passport control is crowded with travelers.

(C) The passengers are waiting to board the plane.

(D) The security checkpoint is full of guards.

---

中文翻譯 (A) 遊客在月台上排隊。

(B) 海關擠滿了旅客。

(C) 旅客等候上機。

(D) 安全檢查站有許多警衛。

解　　答 **(B)**

註　　解

| | | | |
|---|---|---|---|
| tourist | n. 旅客，觀光客 | platform | n. 月臺 |
| passport control | n. 海關 | crowded | a. 擁擠的 |
| traveler | n. 旅客，旅行者 | passenger | n. 乘客 |
| security checkpoint | 安全檢查站 | guard | n. 警衛 |

**10.**

(A) Some visitors are shopping at the boutique.

(B) The fruits are arranged behind the glass display case.

(C) The price labels are placed before the food.

(D) There is a wide selection of desserts on the menu.

---

(A) 一些觀光客正在精品店內購物。　　　　　　 **(C)**

(B) 水果擺放在玻璃展示櫃後面。

(C) 價格標示在食物前面。

(D) 菜單上有很多甜點供選擇。

| boutique | n. 精品店 | arrange | v. 排列 |
|---|---|---|---|
| glass display case | 玻璃展示櫃 | price label | 價錢標籤 |
| wide | a. 廣泛的 | selection | n. 選擇，選項 |

# Part 2 Question & Response

## 「應答問題」的特點與對策

### 題型說明

在這個部份共有 30 題，你會聽到一個問題以及三種不同的回答，問題及三個選項只播放一次，都不會印在試題本上，請針對聽到的內容選擇最適合的答案。

### 基本對策

**1** 本部份每題間隔 5 秒，不須要看任何圖片或文字，只要專心聽。聽的時候，請隨著題號與選項移動筆尖，可在考慮的選項上輕輕點，全部選項聽完，就立刻將決定的答案塗黑，再準備下一題。

**2** 考題大多為「疑問句」，要注意其問話的目的；有的則是「直述句」，陳述事實或看法，考生要從錄音選項中選出最適合的回應。作答時須先注意「疑問詞」，然後是「動詞」、「名詞」部份。

**3** 注意聽疑問詞，必須掌握問句在「問什麼」，問句的形式主要有二：
(1) 以疑問詞為首的問句： who, when, where, why, what (what kind, what day, what time), how (how long, how much, how often, how many years....)
(2) Yes/No 的問句：以助動詞或 be 動詞開頭的問句。
(3) 其他類型：二選一型、附加問句、否定疑問句、直述句⋯等。

**4** 要非常注意發音近似的字，小心選項中的陷阱：近似音字、同音異義字、錯誤時態、人稱不對、答非所問、相同字彙 ( 選項中如果出現與題目相同的字彙時，通常是錯誤的答案 )。

## Part II

**Directions:** You will hear a question or statement and three responses spoken in English. They will be spoken only one time and will not be printed in your test book. Select the best response to the question or statement and mark the letter (A), (B), or (C) on your answer sheet. For example,

You will hear :        Where is the meeting room?

You will also hear :    (A) To meet the new director.

                       (B) It's the first room on the right.   *Sample Answer*

                       (C) Yes, at two o'clock.

The best response to the question "Where is the meeting room?" is choice (B), "It's the first room on the right," so (B) is the correct answer. You should mark answer (B) on your answer sheet.

聽力原文

**11.** Who will be in charge of staff recruiting?

(A) Mr. Cho charged by credit card.

(B) The personnel director hasn't made a decision.

(C) Most employees are recruited from abroad.

**Part 2**

**12.** Have the concierge send up a porter.

(A) But we only have one piece of luggage.

(B) But the port is being renovated.

(C) I'll send you a waiter then.

---

中文翻譯

解 答 **(B)**

**11.** 哪一位負責招募員工？

(A) Cho 先生刷卡付錢。

(B) 人事主管尚未做決定。

(C) 多數員工都從國外招募。

註 解

· be in charge of sth. 負責
· staff recruiting 　職員聘用
· charge 　　　　　用信用卡支付
· personnel director 人事主管
· decision 　　　v. 決定，抉擇
· employee 　　　n. 職員，員工
· recruit 　　　　v. 僱用，招募
· from abroad 　　　從海外

中文翻譯

解 答 **(A)**

**12.** 請服務台派位行李員來。

(A) 可是我們才一件行李而已。

(B) 可是港口正在維修。

(C) 那麼我會派位服務生去。

註 解

· concierge 　　n. 旅館服務台人員
· porter 　　　　n. 行李員，挑夫
· port 　　　　　n. 港口
· renovate 　　　v. 整修

**13.** Could you ask Kenneth to book a roundtrip ticket?

(A) The ticket was cancelled.

(B) He's left for the weekend.

(C) The trip will take around two days.

**14.** What qualifications are you looking for?

(A) An applicant with more experience.

(B) Someone was disqualified from the race.

(C) He looks quite competent.

---

中文翻譯　　　　　　　　　　　　　　　解　答　**(B)**

**13.** 麻煩你請 Kenneth 訂張來回票。

(A) 這張票取消了。　　　　　　　註　解

(B) 他已經離開去度週末了。　　　· book　　　　v. 預訂，預約

(C) 這趟旅程大約要花兩天。　　　· roundtrip ticket　來回票

　　　　　　　　　　　　　　　　· cancel　　　　v. 取消

中文翻譯　　　　　　　　　　　　　　　解　答　**(A)**

**14.** 你要找具備什麼資格的人？

(A) 具有比較豐富經驗的人。　　　註　解

(B) 在比賽中被淘汰的人。　　　· qualification　n. 資格

(C) 他看起來相當有才幹。　　　· applicant　　n. 申請人

　　　　　　　　　　　　　　　· experience　　n. 經驗

　　　　　　　　　　　　　　　· disqualified　　a. 不合格的

　　　　　　　　　　　　　　　· competent　　a. 能幹的

**聽力原文**

**Part 2**

**15.** Will everything be moved to the warehouse?

(A) No, we ran out of silverware.

(B) Yes, I'll have them moved tonight.

(C) But I don't know where the house is.

**16.** What kind of benefit is provided with the offer?

(A) The secretary was kind enough to help.

(B) Their insight would certainly benefit us.

(C) They provide an excellent pension plan.

---

**中文翻譯**

**15.** 所有東西都要搬進倉庫嗎？

(A) 不，我們用完了銀器。

(B) 對，今天晚上我要請人搬。

(C) 可是我不清楚房子在什麼地方。

**解答** **(B)**

**註解**

- warehouse n. 倉庫
- silverware n. 銀器（餐具）
- run out of sth. 用完，耗盡

**中文翻譯**

**16.** 此項提案有什麼好處？

(A) 秘書很好意要幫忙。

(B) 他們的見解必然對我們有利。

(C) 他們提供一個極佳的退休金計畫。

**解答** **(C)**

**註解**

- benefit n. 利益 v. 有利於
- provide v. 提供
- offer n. 報價 v. 提議
- secretary n. 秘書
- insight n. 洞察力；見解
- pension plan 退休金計畫

聽力原文

**17.** What day will the conference be held?

(A) I think following the staff orientation.

(B) It lasted for three days.

(C) Tuesday sounds great!

**18.** The landscape is breathtaking, isn't it?

(A) Those mountains sure look amazing.

(B) The property has dropped in value.

(C) Just take a deep breath.

---

中文翻譯　　　　　　　　　　　　　　　解　答　**(A)**

**17.** 會議要在哪一天舉行？

(A) 我想是在新進員工說明會之後。

(B) 會議為期三天。

(C) 星期二聽起來不錯！

註　解
- conference　n. 會議
- staff orientation
　新進員工說明會
- last　　　v. 延續，為期

中文翻譯　　　　　　　　　　　　　　　解　答　**(A)**

**18.** 這風景真是漂亮啊！

(A) 那些山真的看起來好雄偉。

(B) 房地產價值已經下滑。

(C) 只要深吸一口氣。

註　解
- landscape　　n. 風景
- breathtaking　a. 驚人的
- property　　n. 房地產
- drop　　　v. 掉落，下降
- in value　　價值上
- breath　　　n. 呼吸

**19.** How often are shipments made?

(A) That depends on how many orders we get.

(B) We've boarded the ship twice.

(C) Shipping and handling is free.

**20.** Ms. Kimberly will be resigning from office, won't she?

(A) That's what everyone's saying.

(B) Yes, we got a new design.

(C) This is where the new office will be.

---

中文翻譯

解 答 **(A)**

**19.** 多久運送一次貨物？

(A) 依照所接訂單多寡而定。

(B) 我們已經上船兩次。

(C) 免收運送處理費。

註 解

· shipment　n. 裝載的貨物
· depend on　取決於
· order　n. 訂購
· board　v. 登上
· shipping and handling
　運輸費

中文翻譯

解 答 **(A)**

**20.** Kimberly 女士要離職了，是不是？

(A) 大家都這麼說。

(B) 對啊，我們拿到一個新的設計款。

(C) 這裡是新辦公室的所在地。

註 解

· resign　v. 離職
· design　v. 設計

聽力原文

**21.** Would you like a deluxe suite?

(A) No, I can't have anything sweet.

(B) No, I prefer to have a regular room.

(C) Yes, I'll take it with two sugars.

**22.** Why not post the memo on the bulletin board?

(A) I can't seem to take enough notes.

(B) I'd like to review the content first.

(C) The post office is closed during the holidays.

---

中文翻譯 　　　　　　　　　　　解　答 **(B)**

**21.** 你想要豪華套房嗎？

(A) 不行，我不可以吃甜的東西。

(B) 不，我想要普通房。

(C) 好啊，我要加兩塊方糖。

註　解

· deluxe suite　豪華套房

· regular room　普通房

中文翻譯 　　　　　　　　　　　解　答 **(B)**

**22.** 為何不把公文貼在佈告欄上？

(A) 我好像不能把筆記記得完整。

(B) 我想先看過內容。

(C) 郵局假日不開。

註　解

· post　　　　　v. 貼出

· memo　　　　 n. 備忘錄，公文

· bulletin board 公告欄

· note　　　　　n. 筆記，便條

· review　　　　v. 檢閱

· content　　　　n. 內容

**23.** I guess I'll have to turn down your proposition.

(A) We should turn the radio off.

(B) Can you look it over one more time?

(C) Great! Let's propose a toast!

**Part 2**

**24.** Where can I find the scanner?

(A) They're stored in the computer laboratory.

(B) Just scan the first few pages.

(C) They found the proposal unacceptable.

---

中文翻譯

**23.** 我想我必須退回你的建議案。

(A) 我們應該關掉收音機。

(B) 請你整個再看一遍好嗎？

(C) 太棒了！我們來舉杯慶祝！

解　答 **(B)**

註　解

· proposition　n. 提議
· look it over　　瀏覽
· propose a toast 舉杯祝賀

中文翻譯

**24.** 哪裡有掃描機？

(A) 放在電腦室裡。

(B) 只要掃描前幾頁就好。

(C) 他們發現這個企劃案不可行。

解　答 **(A)**

註　解

· scanner　　n. 掃描機
· store　　　v. 保存
· computer laboratory
　電腦室
· scan　　　v. 掃描
· proposal　n. 提案，企劃案
· unacceptable
　a. 不能接受的

聽力原文

**25.** Do you think earnings will improve this quarter?

(A) Yes, we lost two crates of goods.

(B) Of course, her grades have improved.

(C) We'll have to see how things go.

**26.** What type of account did you open?

(A) A checking account.

(B) It was an open-ended discussion.

(C) You can count on them.

---

中文翻譯

**25.** 你認為這一季的收益會改善嗎？
(A) 是的，我們遺失了兩箱貨物。
(B) 當然啊，她的成績進步了。
(C) 我們還得看情況如何。

解　答 **(C)**

註　解
- earnings　n. 收益
- crate　　n. 條板箱
- goods　　n. 貨物
- grade　　n. 成績
- improve　v. 改善，進步

中文翻譯

**26.** 你開了哪一種帳戶？
(A) 支票帳戶。
(B) 那是開放的討論。
(C) 你可以倚賴他們。

解　答 **(A)**

註　解
- account　　　　n. 帳戶
- checking account 支票帳戶
- open-ended　　a. 開放的
- discussion　　n. 討論
- count on　　　依靠，依賴

聽力原文

**27.** Can you have them prepare an inventory list?

(A) Yes, Raymond invented it.

(B) The phone listing doesn't have our number.

(C) They've already sent one.

**28.** Which computer provides Internet access?

(A) The website has cutting-edge design.

(B) I believe it's accessible by mail.

(C) All except the one in the staff room.

---

中文翻譯

解　答　**(C)**

**27.** 你能請他們準備一份存貨清單嗎？

(A) 對，Raymond 發明的。

(B) 電話名冊上沒有我們的號碼。

(C) 他們已經發出一份。

註　解

· prepare　　　v. 準備
· inventory list　存貨清單
· invent　　　　v. 發明
· phone listing　電話名冊

中文翻譯

解　答　**(C)**

**28.** 哪一台電腦可以上網？

(A) 這個網站有最先進的設計。

(B) 我相信可以透過郵件使用。

(C) 都可以，只有職員室的那台不行。

註　解

· Internet access　　網路使用
· website　　　n. 網站
· cutting-edge　a. 最尖端的
· accessible　　a. 可使用的
· staff room　　　職員室

**29.** Why isn't the intercom working?

(A) Because the job was too difficult.

(B) The technician's testing it.

(C) They no longer offer intercontinental flights.

**30.** Has the firm filed for bankruptcy?

(A) The bank ran out of funds.

(B) No, we'll have to get a filing cabinet.

(C) No, they've found new investors.

---

中 文 翻 譯

解 答 **(B)**

**29.** 對講機怎麼無法操作了？
(A) 因為工作太困難了。
(B) 技術人員正在測試。
(C) 他們不再飛行洲際航班。

註 解

· intercom      n. 對講機
· technician      n. 技術人員
· intercontinental flight
    洲際航班

中 文 翻 譯

解 答 **(C)**

**30.** 這家公司申請破產了嗎？
(A) 這家公司沒有資金了。
(B) 不，我們得拿個檔案櫃。
(C) 不，他們已經找到新的金主。

註 解

· firm      n. 公司，行號
· file for      提出申請
· bankruptcy    n. 破產
· run out of      用盡
· fund      n. 資金
· filing cabinet    檔案櫃
· investor      n. 出資者

**31.** When will the room be available?

(A) Most were unavailable last season.

(B) We still have room for discussion.

(C) Probably not until Monday.

Part

2

**32.** We finally got the green light to start the project.

(A) You should be careful when you are driving.

(B) Mark sure you plan things out carefully.

(C) But I prefer something red or pink.

---

中文翻譯

解　答 **(C)**

**31.** 這房間什麼時候可以使用？

(A) 上一季大部分都沒空。

(B) 我們還有商量的餘地。

(C) 也許要到星期一才可以。

註　解

· available　　a. 有空的，可用的

· unavailable　a. 沒空的

· room　　　　n. 空間

中文翻譯

解　答 **(B)**

**32.** 我們總算獲准開始這項企劃案。

(A) 你開車的時候要小心。

(B) 你一定要謹慎行事。

(C) 但是我比較喜歡紅的或粉紅的。

註　解

· get the green light　被許可

· project　　　　　　n. 企劃案

聽力原文

**33.** Didn't the new merchandise sell like hotcakes?

(A) No, it was Sandra's birthday yesterday.

(B) Yes, everyone enjoyed the cake.

(C) Yes, and now we're out of stock.

**34.** Should I prepare a carbon copy?

(A) Yes, they've moved the photocopy machine.

(B) I don't think that'll be necessary.

(C) Try to remove the stain on the carpet.

---

中文翻譯

**33.** 這項新的商品很暢銷吧？

(A) 不，昨天是 Sandra 的生日。

(B) 對，每個人都很喜歡這個蛋糕。

(C) 對，我們目前缺貨。

解　答 (C)

註　解

· merchandise　　n. 商品
· sell like hotcakes　銷售良好
· out of stock　　無庫存

中文翻譯

**34.** 我需要準備一份副本嗎？

(A) 是，他們已經移走了影印機。

(B) 我想不需要吧。

(C) 想辦法清除地上的髒污。

解　答  (B)

註　解

· carbon copy　n. 副本
· photocopy machine
　影印機
· stain　　　　　n. 汙點，污跡

# QUESTION-RESPONSE

**35.** How much in profit did you make?

(A) Almost twice my initial investment.

(B) She makes profitable use of her time.

(C) Everything comes to a total of $3,000.

**36.** Your evaluation hasn't been received, has it?

(A) No, the crowed was evacuated.

(B) Yes, the receptionist is probably sick.

(C) No, it's supposed to arrive this week.

---

中 文 翻 譯

解　答 **(A)**

**35.** 你賺了多少錢？

(A) 幾乎是當初投資的兩倍。

(B) 她充分有效地利用時間。

(C) 全部總價是三千元。

註　解

- profit　　　　n. 利潤
- initial　　　　a. 最初的
- investment　 n. 投資
- profitable
  a. 有用的，有益的
- total　　　　 n. 總數，總額

中 文 翻 譯

解　答 **(C)**

**36.** 你的評量還沒收到，對嗎？

(A) 不是，群眾都已疏散。

(B) 是的，接待員可能生病了。

(C) 沒有，這個禮拜應該會收到。

註　解

- evaluation　　 n. 評量，評論
- crowed　　　　 n. 人群
- evacuate　　　 v. 疏散
- receptionist　　n. 接待員
- be supposed to V　應該

**37.** How long will negotiations last?

(A) We've longed for this vacation.

(B) The negotiator failed to convince them.

(C) Last time it took two days.

**38.** Who appointed Sarah to handle this project?

(A) Mr. Thompson thought she was suitable.

(B) She prefers a hands-on approach.

(C) Someone left the projector on all night.

---

中文翻譯　　　　　　　　　　　　　解　答　**(C)**

**37.** 會談時間要多久？

(A) 我們很期待這次的假期。

(B) 談判者無法說服他們。

(C) 上一次花了兩天時間。

註　解

· negotiation
　　　　　n. 協商，談判，會議
· long for　　　想要，期盼
· negotiator　n. 交涉者，談判者
· fail to V　　失敗
· convince　　v. 說服

中文翻譯　　　　　　　　　　　　　解　答　**(A)**

**38.** 是誰指派 Sarah 來執行這項企劃案？

(A) Thompson 先生認為她很適合。

(B) 她比較喜歡親自操作的方式。

(C) 有人讓投影機開了一整晚。

註　解

· appoint　　v. 任命
· handle　　　v. 處理
· project　　n. 企劃案
· suitable　　a. 合適的
· hands-on　a. 親自動手的
· approach　n. 方法
· projector　n. 投影機

**39.** May I help you with anything else?

(A) I'd like some napkins.

(B) I'll help you with that.

(C) I'll have it finished soon.

**40.** How could you misplace those articles?

(A) I'm very sorry.

(B) I haven't found a place yet.

(C) I could have read them.

Part

2

---

中文翻譯

解　答 **(A)**

**39.** 還有什麼需要我幫忙的嗎？

(A) 我想要餐巾。

(B) 那件事我會協助你。

(C) 我要趕緊把它完成。

註　解

· napkin  n. 餐巾

中文翻譯

解　答 **(A)**

**40.** 你怎麼會把那些文章放錯？

(A) 真的很抱歉。

(B) 我還沒找到地方。

(C) 我本來可以先看過的。

註　解

· misplace  v. 誤置

· article  　n. 文章

# Part 3 Short Conversations

## 「簡短對話」的特點與對策

### 題型說明

　　這部份共 30 題，你會聽到 10 段兩人的簡短對話，每段對話有三道與對話內容有關的試題，題目會印在試題本上。每題有四個選項，請選擇最適當的答案。對話和試題只播放一次，對話內容不會出現在試題本上。

### 基本對策

**1**　當聽力播放之前或同時，可快速瀏覽題目與選項，邊聽邊找解答。得分關鍵就在於先掃描題目和答案選項，爭取作答時間。

**2**　簡短對話須注意「誰說了什麼」，常見題型有：
(1) 推論情境：答案不在對話內容中，但可由對話情境推論得知。
　　例如：說話者的關係、他們正在做什麼、事情的前因／後果、談話的時間／地點、說話者的職業等。
(2) 主旨題：內容包含地點 (where...)，職業 (who...)，活動 (What be sb doing?)、話題 (What be sb talking about?)... 等。
(3) 細節題：對話中提到的特定細節（人名、地名、價錢、時間等）。或某一位特定說話者（通常是說最後一句話的人）的看法，如 "What does the woman mean? "

## Part III

**Directions:** You will hear some conversations between two people. You will be asked to answer three questions about what the speakers say in each conversation. Select the best response to each question and mark the letter (A), (B), (C), or (D) on your answer sheet. The conversations will be spoken only one time and will not be printed in your test book.

聽力原文　Questions **41-43** refer to the following conversation.

(W) Mr. Sanders and his associates will be expecting our proposal this weedend. Have you finished adding the diagrams?

(M) I've created a few bar graphs for most of our data and included them in the PowerPoint presentation. The flowcharts are almost complete.

(W) Excellent! Make sure you also get extra copies of the proposal made in case they have more people than we anticipate.

(M) Don't worry, I've already asked Janice to prepare 10 copies and also to set up the conference room in advance.

試　題

**41.** What did the man do?
(A) Making 10 copies of the proposal
(B) Producing diagrams
(C) Setting up the conference room
(D) Visiting Mr. Sanders

**42.** What are the speakers preparing for?
(A) A press conference
(B) A meeting presentation
(C) A wedding proposal
(D) A new association

**43.** Where will the meeting most likely take place?
(A) At a local bar
(B) In a conference room
(C) At a convention center
(D) On a computer

中文翻譯

聽力 （女）Sanders 先生和他的同事，要我們這個週末給他們提案報告。你把圖表都加上去了嗎？

（男）我把大部分數據資料都設計了長條圖表，放在投影片上，流程圖也差不多完成了。

（女）很好！記得要多準備幾份企劃書，以防他們來的人數比我們預期的多。

（男）別擔心。我已經請 Janice 準備十份資料，同時也先把會議室安排妥當。

試題 **41.** 男士做好了什麼事情？　　　　　　　　　　解答 **(B)**

(A) 準備十份企劃書

(B) 製作圖表

(C) 安排會議室

(D) 拜訪 Sanders 先生

Part 3

**42.** 兩位談話者在準備什麼事情？　　　　　　　解答 **(B)**

(A) 記者會

(B) 會議報告

(C) 求婚計畫

(D) 新的協會

**43.** 會議可能在何處舉行？　　　　　　　　　　解答 **(B)**

(A) 在當地酒吧

(B) 在會議室

(C) 在會議中心

(D) 透過電腦

註解

| | | | |
|---|---|---|---|
| associate | n. 同事 | expect | v. 指望，期待 |
| proposal | n. 提案，求婚 | diagram | n. 圖表 |
| bar graph | 長條圖 | data | n. 數據 |
| presentation | n. 報告，說明會 | flowchart | n. 流程圖 |
| anticipate | v. 預期 | set up | 準備 |
| conference room | 會議室 | in advance | 預先 |

**聽力原文** Questions **44** through **46** refer to the following conversation.

(M) Hello, this is Kenneth Loewe and I'm one of your Internet service subscribers. My connection's been down for a couple of days and I'm wondering if there's anything wrong with your servers.

(W) Hi, Mr. Lowe, and thank you for calling us. I'll first have to verify your identity. Could you please give me your subscriber ID number, home address, and contact number?

(M) Of course.The ID number on my statement shows K-I-S-2-0-1-5-5-5-4. My home address is 4011 Massachusetts Avenue, Apartment 15, and my home number is 304-833-8458.

(W) Thank you, Mr. Lowe. It shows here that we haven't received your payment for this month and we've also sent out two notices prior to disconnecting your service. If you'd like to clear up the bills now, we can actually just do this over the phone with a credit card, and we'll be able to get your connection back up in twenty minutes. Would you like to do that, sir?

**試　　題**

**44.** What is the purpose of the call?
  (A) To inquire about internet access
  (B) To apply for a credit card
  (C) To register for a membership
  (D) To give personal information

**45.** Why did the woman ask for the man's personal information?
  (A) To input them into a database
  (B) To confirm his identity
  (C) To updata his billing address
  (D) To renew his subscription

**46.** What problem did the man have?
  (A) His phone connection is down.
  (B) His credit card was stolen.
  (C) He can't go online.
  (D) He wants to cancel his service.

中文翻譯

聽力 （男）你好，我叫 Kenneth Lowe，我是你們的網路用戶。我的網路已經斷
　　　　線好幾天了，不知道是不是你們的伺服器有問題？

（女）Lowe 先生，您好，謝謝來電。我必須先跟您核對身分資料。麻煩告訴
　　　我您的用戶號碼，住家地址和聯絡電話。

（男）好的，我帳單上的號碼是 K-I-S-2-0-1-5-5-5-4，住家地址是
　　　Massachusetts 大道 4011 號，15 號公寓，住家電話是 304-833-8458。

（女）謝謝您。Lowe 先生，我這裡的資料顯示，您這個月的費用還未繳交，
　　　在斷線之前，我們已經發出二次通知。如果您現在想要繳清費用，
　　　我們可以馬上透過電話，用信用卡為您處理，二十分鐘後就可以恢
　　　復連線。先生，您要馬上辦嗎？

試題　　**44.** 此通電話的目的為何？　　　　　　　　　解　答　**(A)**
　　　　　　(A) 查詢網路連線
　　　　　　(B) 申請信用卡
　　　　　　(C) 報名會員
　　　　　　(D) 提供個人資料

　　　　　**45.** 女士為何詢問男士的個人資料？　　　　解　答　**(B)**
　　　　　　(A) 要輸入資料庫
　　　　　　(B) 要確認他的身分
　　　　　　(C) 要更新他的帳單地址
　　　　　　(D) 要延展訂閱期

　　　　　**46.** 男士有何問題？　　　　　　　　　　解　答　**(C)**
　　　　　　(A) 他的電話斷線。
　　　　　　(B) 他的信用卡遭竊。
　　　　　　(C) 他無法上網。
　　　　　　(D) 他要取消服務。

Part 3

註　解

| | | | |
|---|---|---|---|
| service subscriber | n. 用戶，訂戶 | connection | n. 連接，連線 |
| down | a. 中斷的 | wonder | v. 納悶 |
| server | n. 伺服器 | verify | v. 核對 |
| identity | n. 身分 | contact number | 聯絡電話 |
| notice | n. 通知，公告 | prior to | 在…之前 |
| disconnect | v. 中斷 | clear up | 償清 |
| bill | n. 帳單 | subscription | n. 訂閱 |

**聽力原文**   Questions **47** through **49** refer to the following conversation.

(M) Good evening. Thank you for calling the Plaza Universal Resort. This is Richard Huang speaking, how may I help you tonight?

(W) Hello, my name is Elaine Thomas, and I'm calling in regard to my room reservation from the nineteenth to the twenty third. I need to postpone my arrival date until the twentieth and I will be checking out on the twenty fifth. I'm also considering upgrading my room. Can you please give me the rate of your luxury suites?

(M) Okey, Ms. Thomas. The rate for our luxury suites is $320.00 for a single night. You'll also get a complimentary breakfast for two and two guest passes to our VIP Sauna and Spa. Would you like to change your room, too?

(W) Sounds great! I'll do that as well.

**試   題**

**47.**   Why did the woman call?
(A)  To book a room
(B)  To cancel a reservation
(C)  To request for a smaller room
(D)  To change a check-in date

**48.**   When will the woman arrive?
(A)  On the nineteenth
(B)  On the twentieth
(C)  On the twenty third
(D)  On the twenty fifth

**49.**   What is the woman likely to do?
(A)  Keep the same room
(B)  Move to a suite
(C)  Get a single room
(D)  Cancel her reservation

中文翻譯

聽力　（男）晚安！感謝您來電 Plaza 寰宇度假飯店。我是 Richard Huang，很高興為您服務！

（女）你好，我是 Elaine Thomas，我要查詢有關我從 19 日到 23 日的訂房。我想要把抵達日期延後到 20 日，然後 25 日退房，還有房間我也想升等。能否告訴我豪華套房是多少價錢？

（男）好的，Thomas 小姐，我們豪華套房一個晚上的價格是 320 元美金，附送二人份的早餐，還有 VIP 桑拿浴和泡湯的使用券二張。您想要更換房間嗎？

（女）好像不錯，我就順便換房間吧！

試題　**47.**　女士為何致電？　　　　　　　　　解答　**(D)**
(A) 要訂房
(B) 要取消訂房
(C) 要求較小的房間
(D) 要變更住房日期

**48.**　女士何時會抵達？　　　　　　　　　解答　**(B)**
(A) 在 19 日
(B) 在 20 日
(C) 在 23 日
(D) 在 25 日

**49.**　女士可能要做何事？　　　　　　　　解答　**(B)**
(A) 保留原有房間
(B) 改住套房
(C) 要單人房
(D) 取消訂房

Part

3

註解

| | | | |
|---|---|---|---|
| resort | n. 度假飯店 | in regard to | 有關 |
| room reservation | 訂房 | postpone | v. 延期 |
| arrival date | 抵達日期 | check out | 退房 |
| upgrade | v. 升級 | rate | n. 價格；費用 |
| luxury suite | 高級套房 | complimentary | a. 免費的；贈送的 |
| guest pass | 賓客通行證 | sauna | n. 桑拿浴；蒸汽浴 |
| spa | n. 溫泉浴 | | |

聽力原文 Questions **50** through **52** refer to the following conversation.

(W) The hotel shuttle should have arrived half an hour ago. Are you sure you have the right schedule?

(M) Well, this was exactly what the tour agent gave me. She said there might be some hold-ups during this time, but the van will definitely turn up. Do you think I should phone them and see if there's anything wrong?

(W) Yes, get in touch with the hotel concierge and see whether we've missed the shuttle or they're just running a bit late. I don't want to end up stranded here at this hour.

(M) Alright then. Maybe we should also check out the car rental service just in case.

試　　題

**50.** What are the speakers waiting for?
(A) A taxicab
(B) A shuttle bus
(C) An express train
(D) A rental car

**51.** What is the problem?
(A) The shuttle is late.
(B) There is no taxi available.
(C) They have the wrong schedule.
(D) They lost the hotel address.

**52.** What does the man suggest?
(A) Ask for the taxi rate
(B) Wait for their ride
(C) Get the hotel address
(D) Visit a car rental service

中文 翻譯

聽 力 （女） 飯店的接駁車半小時前就該來了。你確定你的時刻表是正確的嗎？

（男） 這是旅行社的人給我的呀！她說這個時段有可能延誤，但是小巴士一定會來。你覺得我要不要打電話給他們，問問是怎麼回事？

（女） 對，跟飯店服務台聯絡一下，看看是我們錯過接駁車，還是他們只是來晚了。我可不想這個時候還困在這裡。

（男） 好吧。我們或許也該問問租車公司，以防萬一。

試 題

**50.** 說話者在等候什麼？　　　　　　　　　　　解　　答 **(B)**
　(A) 計程車
　(B) 接駁巴士
　(C) 快速列車
　(D) 出租汽車

**51.** 出了什麼問題？　　　　　　　　　　　　　解　　答 **(A)**
　(A) 接駁車晚到。
　(B) 叫不到計程車。
　(C) 他們的時刻表錯誤。
　(D) 他們遺失飯店地址。

**52.** 男士有何建議？　　　　　　　　　　　　　解　　答 **(D)**
　(A) 詢問計程車費率
　(B) 等人來接
　(C) 取得飯店地址
　(D) 諮詢租車服務

Part 3

註 解

| | | | |
|---|---|---|---|
| hotel shuttle | 飯店接駁車 | schedule | n. 時刻表 |
| tour agent | 旅行社專員 | hold-up | n. 延誤 |
| definitely | adv. 肯定地 | turn up | 出現 |
| get in touch with | 聯絡 | hotel concierge | 旅館服務台 |
| end up | 最後… | stranded | a. 滯留；困住的 |
| check out | 了解狀況 | car rental service | 汽車出租服務 |
| express | a. 高速的，快速的 | | |

聽力原文 Questions **53** through **55** refer to the following conversation.

(M) Excuse me, Sharon. Can you spare a minute? I need to speak with you about the projector screen in the lecture hall.

(W) Sure, Kevin. I had the technician install it last weekend. There's nothing wrong with it, is there?

(M) No, it's perfect. The Director is quite pleased with it and she's planning on setting them up in all the lecture halls. She'd also like to change all the lighting and use brighter illumination. Do you mind giving the technician a call to set up an appointment?

(W) Of course not, I'll drop him a line tomorrow.

試    題

**53.**    Who installed the projector screen?
(A) Sharon
(B) Kevin
(C) The director
(D) A technician

**54.**    What will the woman do tomorrow?
(A) Speak with the director
(B) Install the new screens
(C) Contact the technician
(D) Change the lighting

**55.**    How does the director feel about the new screens?
(A) Satisfied
(B) Disappointed
(C) Excited
(D) Unhappy

中文翻譯

**聽力**

（男）Sharon，對不起，你現在有空嗎？ 我要和你談一下演講廳的放映布幕。

（女）好啊，Kevin，我上週末請技術人員把它安裝上去，沒什麼問題吧？

（男）沒問題，好得很。經理很滿意，而且打算所有演講廳全部安裝。她還想要更換所有的照明設備，改用亮度較高的照明。可以麻煩妳打通電話給技術人員，約個時間嗎？

（女）當然沒問題，我明天就打給他。

**試題**

**53.** 什麼人安裝放映布幕？　　　　　　　　　　**解答** **(D)**
(A) Sharon
(B) Kevin
(C) 經理
(D) 技術人員

**54.** 女士明天會做什麼事？　　　　　　　　　　**解答** **(C)**
(A) 和經理交談
(B) 安裝新的布幕
(C) 聯絡技術人員
(D) 更換照明設備

**55.** 經理對新布幕感覺如何？　　　　　　　　　　**解答** **(A)**
(A) 覺得滿意
(B) 覺得失望
(C) 覺得興奮
(D) 覺得不悅

**註解**

| | | | |
|---|---|---|---|
| spare a minute | 撥空 | projector screen | 投影機布幕 |
| lecture hall | 演講廳 | technician | n. 技術人員 |
| install | v. 安裝 | director | n. 經理，主管 |
| set up | 安裝 | lighting | n. 照明設備 |
| bright | a. 明亮的 | illumination | n. 照明；光亮 |
| appointment | n. 約定 | drop him a line | 打電話給他 |

Part
**3**

Questions **56 through 58** refer to the following conversation.

(W) Hey Michael, did you read the reviews on the latest film?

(M) Not yet, but almost everyone said it got rave reviews, and the critics especially praised the script and the production. It also did very well in the box office, and has been sitting in the number one spot for two consecutive weeks. So Vanessa, do you plan on seeing it?

(W) Well, Tiffany and Daisy saw it last week and they hated it. They thought it was a relief when the credits started rolling. I'll wait for the rental to come out.

(M) I'm surprised to hear that. But it's probably just a matter of personal preference. I'll have to see it for myself tonight, so I'll let you know whether they're right.

試　　題

**56.**　Who isn't going to watch the film?
(A) Michael
(B) Vanessa
(C) Tiffany
(D) Daisy

**57.**　How do critics feel about the movie?
(A) Generally positive.
(B) They hated it.
(C) It was a relief.
(D) Quite negative.

**58.**　What will Vanessa do?
(A) Read the reviews
(B) See the film
(C) Wait for the video
(D) Watch another movie

# SHORT CONVERSATION

**聽力**　（女）嗨，Michael，最近那部新片的影評你看了沒？

（男）還沒看，不過大家都說讚，影評人尤其讚賞劇本和製作。它的票房也很好，已經連續二週都穩居排行榜冠軍。所以，Vanessa，你打算去看嗎？

（女）這個嘛，Tiffany 和 Daisy 上個禮拜看了，他們都覺得很難看，片尾演職員名單出現還覺得謝天謝地。我想還是等出租片出來再看吧。

（男）聽到有人這麼說，我好訝異，不過這可能只是個人喜好的關係。我今天晚上得自己先去看看，我就可以告訴你他們的看法是否正確。

**試題**

**56.** 什麼人不去看電影？　　　　　　　　　**解　答** **(B)**
- (A) Michael
- (B) Vanessa
- (C) Tiffany
- (D) Daisy

**57.** 影評人對此影片看法如何？　　　　　　**解　答** **(A)**
- (A) 大體上正面評價。
- (B) 他們都不喜歡。
- (C) 真是如釋重負。
- (D) 相當負面看法。

**58.** Vanessa 要做什麼事？　　　　　　　　**解　答** **(C)**
- (A) 看影評
- (B) 看影片
- (C) 等影帶出來
- (D) 看另一部電影

Part **3**

**註　解**

| | | | |
|---|---|---|---|
| review | n. 評論 | rave review | 極好的評論 |
| critic | n. 評論家 | praise | v. 讚美 |
| script | n. 腳本 | production | n. 製作 |
| box office | 票房 | number one spot | 第一名 |
| consecutive | a. 連續不斷的 | relief | n. 輕鬆，減輕痛苦 |
| the credits | n. 演職員名單 | roll | v. 轉動；啟動 |
| rental | n. 出租 | personal preference | 個人偏好 |

聽力原文 Questions **59** through **61** refer to the following conversation.

(W) Hello, this is Melissa Hagan. I recently ordered two packs of rechargeable batteries from one of your sales representatives, but the shipment hasn't arrived yet, so I'd like to know what the status of my delivery is.

(M) Hi, Ms. Hagan. I've just pulled your order records and the status shows that the shipment is still 'being delivered.' From what I see, you'll most likely receive the goods this evening or at the latest, tomorrow morning.

(W) That's good to know. I'd also like to inquire about the weekly deals posted on your website. I see there's a free battery recharger after a $40.00 rebate. The disclaimer says that the offer ends on May the 5th, but it's almost the end of the month already.

(M) Oh, I must apologize. There was probably a typo when we posted the weekly deal. The months and days are correct, but the rebate is supposed to be valid until the fifth of next year, not this one. I'll have them correct it right away.

試　　題

**59.** Where is this conversation taking place?
(A) Over the phone
(B) At a meeting
(C) On a website
(D) In a store

**60.** When will the shipment arrive?
(A) Tomorrow morning
(B) Tomorrow evening
(C) On the fifth of May
(D) Next year

**61.** Why did the man apologize?
(A) There was an error on the disclaimer.
(B) The shipment will be late.
(C) The batteries are not working.
(D) The offer is no longer valid.

中文翻譯

聽力 （女）你好，我是 Melissa Hagan。我最近向你們的銷售員訂購了二盒充電式電池，可是一直沒送來，所以我想了解送貨的情形。

（男）Hagan 小姐，你好！我剛看了你的訂購記錄，目前貨品還在運送中。從我所看到的情形，你很可能今天晚上，或者最慢明天早上就會收到。

（女）那就好。我還想問一下，你們張貼在網站上的每週特惠活動。我看到一個扣抵 40 元後免費的電池充電器，說明上面的截止日期是 5 月 5 日，可是現在已經快月底了。

（男）喔，必須跟您說聲抱歉。我們張貼每週特惠活動的時候，可能有打字錯誤。月份和日期部份是正確的，但是折扣有效期間是到明年 5 月，不是今年，我會馬上請人修正。

試題　**59.** 此段對談發生於何處？　　　解 答　**(A)**
(A) 電話中
(B) 會議中
(C) 網站上
(D) 商店內

**60.** 貨運何時送達？　　　解 答　**(A)**
(A) 明天上午
(B) 明天晚上
(C) 5 月 5 日
(D) 明年

**61.** 男士為何要致歉？　　　解 答　**(A)**
(A) 說明上有錯誤。
(B) 貨運會晚到。
(C) 電池故障。
(D) 報價已失效。

Part **3**

註 解

| | | | |
|---|---|---|---|
| order | v. 訂購 | rechargeable battery | 可充電電池 |
| sales representative | 銷售員 | status | n. 狀態 |
| delivery | n. 郵寄，運送 | inquire about | 詢問 |
| post | v. 張貼訊息 | battery recharger | 電池充電器 |
| rebate | n. 折扣，貼現，減免額 | disclaimer | n. 聲明 |
| typo | n. 打字錯誤 | deal | n. 特價 |
| offer | n. 報價 | valid | a. 有效的 |

聽力原文 Questions **62** through **64** refer to the following conversation.

(W) I'm sorry to hear what happened at the meeting, Jennifer. I hope you're not upset.

(M) Not really. Initially I thought Mr. Cooper's evaluation was biased and harsh. But after I read his written comments, I realized that his accusations aren't groundless, and the truth is my team had consistently put the blame on external factors such as bad fortune or the slow economy.

(W) Do you mean to say you agree with his observations?

(M) I'll have to say he's right on the mark. And I'm glad that's the case, because it'll draw my attention back to the basics of leading my team and finding solutions to the problems we've had throughout.

試 題

**62.** What happened to the woman?
(A) She was fired.
(B) She was criticized.
(C) She got a promotion.
(D) She missed her meeting.

**63.** What is probably the woman's job position?
(A) A board member
(B) An economist
(C) A team leader
(D) An observer

**64.** How does the woman feel about Mr. Cooper's evaluation?
(A) Groundless
(B) Constructive
(C) Meaningless
(D) Useless

**中文翻譯**

**聽 力** （男）Jennifer，會議上發生的事情我聽說了，我很難過。希望妳不要太傷心才好。

（女）也不會啦。最初我是覺得 Cooper 先生的評估報告有偏見、太過嚴苛。可是我看了他所寫的評論之後，我發覺他的指控也並非毫無根據。而事實上我的團隊只是一直把所有過錯怪罪到外在的因素，像是運氣不佳，或是景氣太差等等。

（男）你的意思是說妳同意他的觀察囉？

（女）我必須承認他說的都對，而且我覺得慶幸，因為這樣可以把我的注意力拉回到領導團隊的基本面，針對我們所面臨的問題找到解決的方法。

**試 題**

**62.** 女士發生了什麼事？　　　　　　　　　**解 答** **(B)**
(A) 她被解雇。
(B) 她受到批評。
(C) 她獲得升遷。
(D) 她錯過會議。

**63.** 女士的職務可能為何？　　　　　　　　**解 答** **(C)**
(A) 董事
(B) 經濟學者
(C) 團隊領導人
(D) 觀察員

**64.** 女士對 Cooper 先生的評估有何看法？　**解 答** **(B)**
(A) 毫無根據
(B) 有建設性
(C) 毫無意義
(D) 無用處的

Part **3**

**註 解**

| | | | | |
|---|---|---|---|---|
| initially | adv. 最初地 | evaluation | n. 評估報告，估價 |
| biased | a. 有偏見的，不公平 | harsh | a. 嚴厲的 |
| comment | n. 批評，評論 | realize | v. 了解 |
| accusation | n. 指控 | groundless | a. 毫無根據的 |
| consistently | adv. 一貫地 | put the blame on | 歸咎於 |
| external | a. 外界的 | factor | n. 因素 |
| fortune | n. 運氣 | economy | n. 經濟 |
| observation | n. 觀察 | on the mark | 正確的 |
| basics | n. 基礎，基本原則 | solution | n. 解答 |

聽力原文　Questions **65** through **67** refer to the following conversation.

(M1) Sorry, Michael, are you done looking at the accounts of Edinburgh Property Management? This audit needs to be concluded before Friday and I fear we're running a bit behind schedule.

(M2) Most of the work has been done, but I still need to speak with their bookkeepers this Tuesday over some discrepancy in their third quarter profit statements. It seems that a few of their apartment units haven't been occupied for over two quarters, but the loss was written off and somehow it shows a profit in their annual report. Any thoughts?

(M1) Recheck the records to confirm the numbers and give me an update before Thursday.

(M2) Alright. Hopefully this is just an oversight on my part.

試　　題

**65.** What does Michael plan to do?
(A) Postpone a report
(B) Speak with bookkeepers
(C) Call the accounting director
(D) Visit the apartment units

**66.** What are the speakers mainly talking about?
(A) An accounting director
(B) A profit estimate
(C) Apartment units
(D) An audit report

**67.** When is the deadline for the audit?
(A) Today
(B) Tuesday
(C) Friday
(D) Saturday

**中文翻譯**

**聽力**

（男 1）Michael，不好意思，你是不是已經看完 Edinburgh 資產管理公司的帳目？審計工作得在星期五以前完成，我怕我們的進度有點落後了。

（男 2）大部分工作都完成了，但是我星期二還得和他們的帳務人員談談，針對一些第三季盈利報表上的誤差。看起來，他們有些公寓已經二季以上沒有使用，可是虧損都勾銷掉，而且不知怎麼回事，在年度報告上還出現盈餘。關於這點你有何看法？

（男 1）重新再核對記錄，確認數目，星期四以前交給我最新資料。

（男 2）好的。希望純粹是我個人的疏忽。

**試題**

**Part 3**

**65.** Michael 打算做什麼？　　　　　　　　　　解 答 **(B)**
(A) 延後交報告
(B) 和帳務人員談談
(C) 致電會計主任
(D) 去看公寓房子

**66.** 談話者主要在談論什麼？　　　　　　　　　解 答 **(D)**
(A) 某一位會計主管
(B) 某一筆獲利評估
(C) 公寓房子
(D) 某一份審計報告

**67.** 審計工作截止日是哪一天？　　　　　　　　解 答 **(C)**
(A) 今天
(B) 週二
(C) 週五
(D) 週六

**註 解**

| | | | |
|---|---|---|---|
| account | n. 帳戶，帳目 | audit | n. 查帳，審計 |
| conclude | v. 結束 | bookkeeper | n. 帳務人員 |
| discrepancy | n. 不一致，誤差 | profit statement | 盈利報表 |
| apartment unit | 公寓單位 | occupy | v. 佔用 |
| loss | n. 虧損 | write off | 註銷；勾銷 |
| annual report | 年度報告 | oversight | n. 疏忽出錯 |

Questions **68** through**70** refer to the following conversation.

(M) Hi Melanie, can I have a minute? I need to speak to you about the stock analysis you did on KCR Electronics.

(W) Sure, Steve. What's the problem?

(M) You remember Olson Williams from accounting, right? He advised us to take into account the recent scandal at KCR. And I've got word that KCR's latest line of products will most likely be delayed because of some technical glitches.

(W) Now that you mention it, I really ought to redo this review.

**68.** What do the speakers most likely do?
(A) Electronic engineers
(B) Stock analysts
(C) Accountants
(D) Production managers

**69.** What does the man suggest the woman do?
(A) Fix the technical glitches
(B) Give him some change
(C) Take another look at her analysis
(D) Speak to an accountant

**70.** What type of business does KCR probably do?
(A) Bank accounts
(B) Stock exchange
(C) Electronic products
(D) Technical advice

# SHORT CONVERSATION

**聽力**（男）嗨，Melanie，有空嗎？我得和妳談談妳對 KCR 電子公司所作的股票分析。

（女）好的，Steve，有什麼問題嗎？

（男）妳還記得會計部的 Olson Williams 吧？他建議我們要考量到 KCR 最近的醜聞。而且我得到消息，KCR 最近推出的系列產品，由於某些技術上的瑕疵，很可能延誤上市。

（女）既然你這麼說，我真的該重作評估。

**試題** **68.** 談話者可能從事何種工作？　　　　　　　　**解 答 (B)**
(A) 電子工程師
(B) 股票分析師
(C) 會計人員
(D) 生產經理

**Part 3**

**69.** 男士建議女士何事？　　　　　　　　**解 答 (C)**
(A) 修復技術上的小毛病
(B) 給他一些零錢
(C) 再度審視分析內容
(D) 和會計人員談談

**70.** KCR 的營業項目為何？　　　　　　　　**解 答 (C)**
(A) 銀行帳目
(B) 證券交易
(C) 電子產品
(D) 技術指導

**註 解**

| stock analysis | 股票分析 | accounting | n. 會計部門 |
|---|---|---|---|
| advise | v. 建議 | take into account | 考慮到 |
| recent | a. 最近的 | scandal | n. 醜聞 |
| word | n. 消息 | line of products | 產品系列 |
| delay | n. 延誤 | glitch | n. 小故障，小毛病 |
| redo | v. 再做 | review | n. 評論 |

# Part 4 Short Talks

## 「簡短獨白」的特點與對策

**Part IV**
**Directions:** You will hear some conversations between two people. You will be asked to answer three questions about what the speakers say in each conversation. Select the best response to each question and mark the letter (A), (B), (C), or (D) on your answer sheet. The conversations will be spoken only one time and will not be printed in your test book.

## 題型說明

　　這個部份共有 30 題，你會聽到 10 段簡短獨白，每段獨白內容對應三道試題，題目會印在試題本上。每題有四個選項，請從其中選出最適當的答案。每段獨白和試題只播放一次，獨白內容不會印在試題本上。

## 基本對策

**1**　此部份每題間隔 8 秒。得分秘訣就是利用一開始聽說明的時間，搶先預覽題目與選項，每組三題，快速作答，再利用省下來的時間，再準備下一個題組。

**2**　答案選項在獨白中都可能出現，須注意簡短獨白開頭的介紹，可以幫助快速理解該獨白內容，辨別題型。常考的文章類型有廣播、新聞、氣象報告、廣告、語音留言⋯等。

**3**　作答時記得用「刪除法」，同時輕輕點可能的答案，聽完整段再確認答案。正確答案常以同義字出現。

**4**　此部份對考生最大的挑戰是字彙與速度，是聽力測驗中最難的部份，但也可視為作閱讀的準備。練習時要多開口跟讀，才能用聲音記單字，了解字義，更要會唸、會聽。

Questions **71** through **73** refer to the following talk.

Hello, everyone. Today I'm going to give you a brief overview of our tour. First, we'll set out from Chapel Bridge, which is Lucerne's main landmark. The bridge was constructed in 1333, and was virtually destroyed by a fire on August 18, 1993. After we cross the bridge, we'll pass several plazas on the riverside. Then we'll proceed to the Musegg Wall. Unfortunately, the wall is only accessible to the visitors during the summer. After the Musegg Wall, we're going to hit the Lion Plaza, where the Lion Monument lies.

試　　題

**71.** What is the main landmark?
(A) The Lion Monument
(B) The Lion Plaza
(C) The Chapel Bridge
(D) Lucerne

**72.** What does the speaker say about the Monument?
(A) It was destroyed by a fire.
(B) It is only accessible during the summer.
(C) It was built in 1333.
(D) It is located in the Lion Plaza.

**73.** Which place can NOT be visited in winter?
(A) The Musegg Wall
(B) The Lucerne
(C) The Lion Monument
(D) The Chapel Bridge

**中文翻譯**

請參考以下的談話：

　　大家好！今天我要給各位簡介我們的行程。首先，我們會先從教堂大橋出發，它是 Lucerne 主要的地標。這座橋於西元 1333 年建造，曾在 1993 年 8 月 18 日差點在一場大火中付之一炬。走過大橋之後，我們會經過河岸邊的幾個廣場，然後前往 Musegg 城牆。很不巧的是，這道城牆只有在夏季才開放給遊客參觀。經過 Musegg 城牆以後，我們就會來到獅子廣場，就是獅子紀念碑的所在地。

**試題**

**71.** 哪裡是主要地標？　　　　　　　　　　　　　**解答 (C)**
(A) 獅子紀念碑
(B) 獅子廣場
(C) 教堂大橋
(D) Lucerne

**72.** 關於紀念碑，說話者說了什麼？　　　　　　　**解答 (D)**
(A) 被大火焚毀。
(B) 只能在夏季參觀。
(C) 建於 1333 年。
(D) 位於獅子廣場。

**Part 4**

**73.** 哪個地方在冬季無法參觀？　　　　　　　　　**解答 (A)**
(A) Musegg 城牆
(B) Lucerne
(C) 獅子紀念碑
(D) 教堂大橋

**註解**

| | | | |
|---|---|---|---|
| brief | a. 簡短的 | overview | n. 總覽 |
| set out | 出發 | chapel | n. 教堂，禮拜堂 |
| landmark | n. 地標 | construct | v. 建造 |
| virtually | adv. 差不多，實際上 | destroy | v. 破壞，毀壞 |
| proceed | v. 前進 | accessible | a. 可接近的 |
| monument | n. 紀念碑 | | |

聽力原文　Questions **74** through **76** refer to the following annoucement.

Good morning, shoppers. Thank you for shopping with us. While you're here, don't miss our "Specialty Center," where our Swiss Festival is currently being held. There you'll find all of your favorite Swiss souvenirs, from watches, koo-koo clocks, music boxes, Swiss army knives, jewelry, and fine chocolates, all imported directly from Switzerland. We're also giving away free gifts for purchases over $30.00! And on top of that, you can pick up a free lottery ticket at the service counter and enter into our weekly draw. The winner will be given two first-class roundtrip tickets to Switzerland, along with a $500.00 gift certificate to any of our outlets!

試　　題

**74.** What is this announcement for?
(A) To thank customers
(B) To promote a sales campaign
(C) To advertise a new product
(D) To present a shopping center

**75.** What does the specialty center sell this week?
(A) Tulips from Holland
(B) French wine
(C) Swiss chocolate
(D) Festival decorations

**76.** What does the speaker say about the center?
(A) It is located in Switzerland.
(B) It is free of charge.
(C) It is a single room.
(D) It sells various goods.

**中文翻譯**

請參考以下的廣播：

　　各位顧客，早安！謝謝光臨本公司！提醒您在此購物時，千萬別錯過我們的「特產名品中心」，現在正在舉辦瑞士節慶活動。在那裡可以看到所有您喜愛的瑞士紀念品，從手錶、咕咕鐘、音樂盒、瑞士刀、珠寶飾品以及巧克力等等，都是由瑞士直接進口。只要購物滿美金 30 元，我們還有贈品。最棒的是，您可以在服務台領取一張免費樂透彩券，參加我們的週週送抽獎活動，有機會抽中兩張瑞士來回的頭等艙機票，還有 500 元禮券送給您，可以在我們所有的暢貨中心使用。

**試題**

**74.** 本段廣播目的為何？　　　　　　　　　　**解 答 (B)**
(A) 向顧客致謝
(B) 促銷活動
(C) 廣告新產品
(D) 介紹購物中心

**75.** 特產名品中心本週販售什麼商品？　　　　**解 答 (C)**
(A) 荷蘭來的鬱金香
(B) 法國的紅酒
(C) 瑞士巧克力
(D) 節慶飾品

**76.** 關於中心，說話者說了什麼？　　　　　　**解 答 (D)**
(A) 它位於瑞士
(B) 它是免付費的
(C) 它是單人房
(D) 它販售多樣商品

**Part 4**

**註 解**

| | | | |
|---|---|---|---|
| specialty | n. 特產，特色（菜） | festival | n. 節慶 |
| purchase | n./v. 購物，採買 | lottery | n. 樂透，抽獎 |
| draw | n. 抽出，抽獎 | roundtrip | n. 來回 / 往返旅程 |
| gift certificate | 禮券 | outlet | n. 暢貨中心 |
| advertise | v. 廣告 | various | a. 多樣的，不同的 |

Questions **77** through **79** refer to the following talk.

Tonight we honor Kimberly K. Roberts, who has given a $5 million gift to the Pinker's Free Children's Hospital to establish a new cancer research center. We thank Ms. Roberts for her generous gift to our hospital. In a time of declining government funding for programs that benefit the disadvantaged, NPOs such as our hospital must work harder than ever to encourage philanthropy and gather as much support as possible from everyone. I am very proud to say that, tonight, we have taken another step forward in achieving that goal. We thank Ms. Roberts again, and hope her spirit and affection will spread to each and every one of us.

試　　題

**77.** What kind of event is the talk taking place at?
(A) A charity banquet
(B) A community assembly
(C) A government meeting
(D) A research seminar

**78.** Who is Kimberly K. Roberts?
(A) A hospital director
(B) A benefactor
(C) A fundraiser
(D) A community organizer

**79.** What does the speaker imply about the government?
(A) It has reached out to disadvantaged children.
(B) It has been involved with the ounding of the hospital.
(C) It has reduced financial support to charity groups.
(D) It has been promoting values of philanthropy.

中文翻譯

請參考以下的談話：

　　今天晚上我們要向 Kimberly K. Roberts 女士表達敬意，她捐贈了一份五百萬美元的大禮給 Pinker 自由兒童醫院，設立新的癌症研究中心。我們非常感謝 Roberts 女士慷慨捐贈給本院。在這政府贊助弱勢團體專案的基金減少的時候，像我們醫院這樣的非營利機構就必須比以往更加賣力，鼓勵大家多多行善，才能集結眾人之力支持下去。今天晚上我要很驕傲地告訴各位，我們又向目標邁進了一大步。再次感恩 Roberts 女士，希望她的慈愛精神會感染我們在座的每一位。

試題　**77.** 本段致詞是在什麼場合所說的？　　　　解　答　**(A)**
　　　　(A) 慈善宴會
　　　　(B) 社區大會
　　　　(C) 政府會議
　　　　(D) 研究討論會

**78.** Kimberly K. Roberts 是什麼人？　　　　解　答　**(B)**
　　　　(A) 醫院主任
　　　　(B) 慈善家
　　　　(C) 募款者
　　　　(D) 社區規劃員

Part
4

**79.** 致詞者對於政府有何說法？　　　　解　答　**(C)**
　　　　(A) 對弱勢兒童伸出援手。
　　　　(B) 參與醫院的創立。
　　　　(C) 減少對慈善團體的金援。
　　　　(D) 提昇善舉的價值。

註　解

| | | | |
|---|---|---|---|
| honor | v. 表敬意，表揚 | establish | v. 設立 |
| research center | 研究中心 | generous | a. 慷慨的 |
| decline | v. 衰退 | funding | n. 資金 |
| benefit | v. 使受惠，有益於 | the disadvantaged | 弱勢團體 |
| NPO (nonprofit organization) 非營利機構 | | encourage | v. 鼓勵 |
| philanthropy | n. 慈善行為，善舉 | achieve | v. 實現 |
| spirit | n. 精神 | affection | n. 關愛 |
| spread | v. 散佈 | charity | n. 慈善 |

聽力原文 Questions **80** through **82** refer to the following talk.

Good evening, listeners. Welcome back to the "The Night of Symphony". I'm Steven Miller, your host. Coming up next is "The First Moment of Symphony" performed by the New York Philharmonic. Back in 1842, the New York Philharmonic was founded by several local musicians under Ureli Corelli Hill's leadership. To date the New York Philharmonic has become one of the oldest orchestras in the world. The orchestra started its first tour in 1882. Each season, music lovers in every corner around the globe are granted the beauty and diversity of classical music through the frequent tours of the orchestra. On average, it gives 180 performances each year. Currently, the New York Philharmonic is on its tour, and our city is its next stop. We'll be giving away 10 tickets to the first performance in our city. Please write us for more information and you'll have a chance to become a lucky winner.

**80.** Where can this talk probably be heard?
(A) In a lecture
(B) At a conference
(C) On the radio
(D) In the news

**81.** What is mentioned about the orchestra?
(A) It was founded in 1882.
(B) It has very few performances each year.
(C) It travels a lot around the world.
(D) Its musicians are from different countries.

**82.** How should listeners obtain the free tickets?
(A) By mail
(B) By phone
(C) By email
(D) Go online

中文翻譯

請參考以下的談話：

　　各位聽眾晚安！歡迎繼續收聽「交響樂之夜」，我是主持人 Steven Miller。接下來為您安排播出的是由紐約愛樂管絃樂團所演出的〝交響曲第一樂章〞。早在 1842 年，紐約當地的一些音樂家在希爾 (Ureli Corelli Hill) 的帶領下，成立了紐約愛樂管絃樂團，至今已成為全球歷史最悠久的古典樂團之一。紐約樂團自 1882 年開始作巡迴演出，每一季透過巡迴演出，和世界各地的樂迷分享優美而多元的古典音樂。一般來說，每一年有 180 場演出。目前樂團正在各地巡迴，下一站即將來到本地。我們有十張本市首演的門票要贈送給大家。歡迎聽眾來函索取詳細資料，您就有機會成為幸運得主！

試題 **80.** 此段談話可能在何處聽到？　　解答 **(C)**
(A) 講課時
(B) 會議中
(C) 收音機
(D) 新聞上

**81.** 談話中提及樂團什麼事？　　解答 **(C)**
(A) 它成立於 1882 年。
(B) 每年演出場次很少。
(C) 它經常巡迴世界各地。
(D) 樂團成員來自不同國家。

Part
4

**82.** 聽眾應該如何取得贈票？　　解答 **(A)**
(A) 用信件
(B) 打電話
(C) 寄 e-mail
(D) 上網

註　解

| | | | |
|---|---|---|---|
| symphony | n. 交響樂 | perform | v. 演出，演奏 |
| philharmonic | n. 管絃樂團 | orchestra | n. 樂隊，樂團 |
| diversity | n. 多元化 | frequent | a. 經常的 |
| on average | 一般來說 | give away | 贈送，送出 |

Questions **83 through 85** refer to the following talk.

Thank you all, my fellow colleagues, for this wonderful surprise before I spend my last day as your Director of Marketing. The past 20 years have been like a roller coaster ride. We've had our ups and downs, successes and failures, and all of which have made us laugh out loud or pull out our hair. And it has been this experience that somehow drew each and every one of us in this department closer, making us not only associates, but family as well. I remember when we first began with only three people in this department, with nothing but a simple drive to do all we can. And that very day when I was placed in charge 12 years ago. Today there are 50 of you standing in this room. And this will not end here. After tomorrow, you will continue to strive and succeed.

試　　題

**83.** Who is the speaker?
(A) A roller coaster designer
(B) A sales associate
(C) A department head
(D) A movie director

**84.** What is the purpose of this talk?
(A) To describe a family
(B) To bid farewell
(C) To join a department
(D) To welcome a new director

**85.** How long has the speaker been with the firm?
(A) Three years
(B) Twelve years
(C) Twenty years
(D) Fifty years

中文翻譯

請參考以下的談話：

感謝各位同事，在我擔任你們的行銷部經理的最後一天給我這麼美好的驚喜。過去這二十年來彷彿在坐雲霄飛車，我們有起有落，有成功，有失敗，還有許許多多讓我們大聲歡笑或是憤怒懊惱的事。這一切的一切卻讓部門裡的每一位同仁更加親密，我們不只是同事關係，也像家人一樣。我記得剛開始部門裏僅有三個人，我們有的就只是一股幹勁，大家賣力往前衝。我也還記得 12 年前被指派來當主管的那一天，而今天站在這裡的人，已有五十位之多了。而這一切不會到此結束，明天之後，大家還是要繼續打拼、努力成功！

試題

**83.** 致詞者是何人？　　　　　　　　　　　　　　　解答 **(C)**
(A) 雲霄飛車設計師
(B) 銷售員
(C) 部門主管
(D) 電影導演

**84.** 此段談話目的為何？　　　　　　　　　　　　　解答 **(B)**
(A) 描述一個家庭
(B) 致告別詞
(C) 加入一個部門
(D) 歡迎新任經理

**85.** 致詞者在公司任職多久？　　　　　　　　　　　解答 **(C)**
(A) 3 年
(B) 12 年
(C) 20 年
(D) 50 年

Part

**4**

註　解

| colleague | n. 同事 | roller coaster | 雲霄飛車 |
| failure | n. 失敗 | experience | n. 經驗 |
| draw | v. 拉 | associate | n. 同事；夥伴 |
| drive | n. 幹勁 | in charge | 負責 |
| strive | v. 奮鬥 | | |

Questions **86** through **88** refer to the following talk.

It is my pleasure to report that our sales figures and turnover for Charmed Perfume have improved dramatically over the last year. With total revenue of 9 million dollars, we have surpassed our target of 7 million dollars. Currently we estimate that, assuming the economy remains stable and there are no other problems, our sales growth will rise by at least another 10%. Furthermore, if our new line of cosmetics is introduced in time for the holiday season, the numbers will run even higher; we roughly estimate about 12 million dollars. In conclusion, let's look forward to another profitable year. Please feel free to ask any questions you might have regarding the report we've given you.

試　　題

**86.** Where is this talk probably taking place?
(A) At a product presentation
(B) At a perfume exhibit
(C) At a corporate meeting
(D) At a cosmetics store

**87.** How much is the total revenue?
(A) 7 million dollars
(B) 9 million dollars
(C) 10 million dollars
(D) 12 million dollars

**88.** What can be implied about the team's performance this year?
(A) Right on target
(B) Surpassing expectations
(C) Poorer than anticipated
(D) Unforeseen failures

# SHORT TALKS

請參考以下的談話：

很高興跟各位報告，在過去這一年來「迷人香水」Charmed Perfume 的銷售數字和營業額有大幅度的進步，總收益達九百萬美元，已經超過原先七百萬美元的目標。目前我們估計，假如經濟保持穩定，也沒有發生其他問題的話，我們的業績至少會再成長十個百分點。還有，如果我們新的化妝品系列及時在假期間推出，數字還會上漲更多，約略估計可達一千二百萬美元左右。總而言之，讓我們期待另一個豐收的一年。對於發給各位的報告，如果有任何疑問的話，請儘量提出來。

**試題**

**86.** 此段談話可能發生於何處？　　**解答 (C)**
(A) 產品介紹會
(B) 香水展覽
(C) 公司會報
(D) 化妝品店

**87.** 總收入有多少？　　**解答 (B)**
(A) 七百萬美元
(B) 九百萬美元
(C) 一千萬美元
(D) 一千二百萬美元

**88.** 今年團隊的表現如何？　　**解答 (B)**
(A) 達成目標
(B) 超越預期
(C) 不如預期
(D) 無預期的失敗

**註解**

| | | | |
|---|---|---|---|
| pleasure | n. 愉悅，樂趣 | sales figure | 銷售數字 |
| turnover | n. 營業額，銷售量 | dramatically | adv. 驚人地，戲劇性地 |
| revenue | n. 收入，收益 | surpass | v. 超越 |
| target | n. 目標 | estimate | v. 估計 |
| assume | v. 假定為 | economy | n. 經濟 |
| stable | a. 穩定的 | line | n. 系列 |
| cosmetics | n. 化妝 / 美容用品 | introduce | v. 推出 |
| roughly | n. 大約 | conclusion | n. 結論 |
| profitable | a. 有利潤的 | anticipate | v. 預期；預料 |

Part 4

Questions **89** through **91** refer to the following talk.

Good evening, and welcome to this book signing session here at the Greentree Auditorium. Tonight I'll be sharing some of the details about my new book, "*The Complete Q&A to Business Success*," which, thanks to your support, has been the number one best-seller. Many of you have asked me how I came to write this book. Well, before I wrote the book, I had sold all my businesses and wondered about what I wanted to do next. I knew I've always wanted to teach. At the same time, I wanted to help businesses succeed. I outlined a list of questions that are most often asked: How do we shape our corporate identity? How do we stay competitive? Essentially, all these questions have to do with approach. So, rather than formulating a theory, I decided to craft an instruction manual of sorts, with a list of potential solutions to familiar issues that businesses face.

試　　題

**89.** What is the speaker's present occupation?
(A) School teacher
(B) Publisher
(C) Author
(D) Business owner

**90.** Where is this talk taking place?
(A) In a bookstore
(B) In an auditorium
(C) In a business center
(D) In a classroom

**91.** What is true about the book?
(A) It is an autobiography of the author.
(B) It instructs people how to apply teaching approaches.
(C) It is a reference manual for business executives.
(D) It provides client and customer listing.

# SHORT TALKS

　　大家晚安，歡迎來到 Greentree 會堂，參加這一場簽書會。今天晚上我要來與大家分享我這本新書《商場致勝 Q&A 全集》的一些細節。幸虧各位的支持，這本書已登上銷售排行榜冠軍。在座有很多人都問我怎麼會寫這本書。這麼說吧，在我動手寫這本書之前，我賣掉我所有的產業，也一直在想下一步我要做什麼。我知道自己一直很想做教學工作，同時，我也想幫助企業界成功。我概列出最常被問到的問題，例如：我們要如何定位公司特性？我們要如何保持競爭力？從本質上說，這些問題都必須用方法解決，所以與其光談理論，我決定創造一本教戰手冊，包含各種企業常會面對的問題的可能解決方案。

**試題**

**89.** 說話者目前的職業為何？　　　　　　　　　**解答 (C)**
(A) 學校教師
(B) 出版商
(C) 作者
(D) 企業老闆

**90.** 此段談話在何處發生？　　　　　　　　　　**解答 (B)**
(A) 在書店內
(B) 在會堂裏
(C) 在商業中心
(D) 在教室裏

**91.** 關於此書何者為真？　　　　　　　　　　　**解答 (C)**
(A) 這是作者的自傳。
(B) 它指導大眾如何運用教學方法。
(C) 這是給企業經營者的參考手冊。
(D) 它提供客戶名單。

**Part 4**

**註解**

| | | | |
|---|---|---|---|
| book signing session | 簽書會 | auditorium | n. 會堂，大禮堂 |
| best-seller | n. 銷售第一 | wonder about | 想知道 |
| outline | v. 列出綱要 | corporate identity | 公司特性 / 定位 |
| competitive | a. 有競爭力的 | essentially | adv. 本質上 |
| approach | n. 方法 | formulate | v. 規劃 |
| theory | n. 理論 | craft | v. 創造 |
| instruction manual | 指導手冊 | potential | a. 潛在的，可能的 |
| solution | n. 解答 | familiar | a. 熟悉的 |

Questions **92** through **94** refer to the following news report.

In today's news, the legislature has passed a new federal law banning businesses from offering lump-sum pensions to retiring employees. The new law will apply to businesses with pension plans that are more than 30% underfinanced. Lawmakers believe that this will discourage businesses from drawing funds out of employee pensions when they need additional capital or another source of funds. Though most businesses believe the law will not have much of an effect on their everyday operations or overall finances, many employees fear that their pension plans may be slashed or affected. The new law will come into effect starting January 1st next year, and will affect more than 60,000 prospective retirees. Stay tuned for an in-depth analysis with Peter Rogers and Richard Wheal.

試　　題

**92.** What is the message mainly about?
(A) Retirement tips
(B) A restriction
(C) Pension for lawmakers
(D) Business finance

**93.** Who is most worried about the new law?
(A) Lawmakers
(B) Business owners
(C) Prospective retirees
(D) Business customers

**94.** What will happen on January 1st?
(A) A new law will be proposed.
(B) Retirees will receive their pension.
(C) A regulation will come into effect.
(D) Lawmakers will lift the ban.

中文翻譯

今天的新聞報導，立法單位通過了一項新的聯邦法律，禁止企業將退休金一次發給退休員工。這項新的法令會適用於退休資金 30% 以上短缺的公司。立法人員認為，如此一來可以讓公司在需要額外資金或是其他資金來源的時候，不會再抽用員工退休預備金。雖然大多數企業相信這項法令不足以影響到他們日常的營運，或是整體的財務狀況，可是很多員工都擔心他們的退休方案會因此而縮水或受影響。這項新法令將在明年元旦生效，會有六萬多位預定退休的員工受到影響。歡迎待會兒繼續收聽 Peter Rogers 和 Richard Wheal 所作的深入分析。

試題

**92.** 此項訊息主要與何事有關？　　解答 **(B)**
(A) 退休建議
(B) 限定、規範
(C) 立法人員的退休金
(D) 企業財務

**93.** 什麼人最擔心此項新法令？　　解答 **(C)**
(A) 立法人員
(B) 企業老闆
(C) 預定退休人員
(D) 公司客戶

Part 4

**94.** 元月一日將發生何事？
(A) 新法令提付表決。　　解答 **(C)**
(B) 退休人員領到退休金。
(C) 一項法規將生效。
(D) 立法人員將撤銷禁令。

註解

| | | | |
|---|---|---|---|
| legislature | n. 立法機關 | federal | a. 聯邦政府的 |
| ban | v. 禁止 | lump-sum | n. 一次付款額 |
| pension | n. 退休金 | underfinanced | a. 資金短缺的 |
| lawmaker | n. 立法者 | discourage | v. 防止 |
| capital | n. 資本 | source | n. 來源 |
| operation | n. 營運 | overall | a. 大體上 |
| finances | n. (用複數)財務狀況 | slash | v. 減少 |
| come into effect | 生效 | prospective | a. 預期的 |
| stay tuned | 繼續收聽 | in-depth | a. 深入的 |
| analysis | n. 分析 | lift the ban | 解除禁令 |

Questions **95** through **97** refer to the following messgage.

Hello, Mr. Albertson. This is Laurence Wilco calling from Systel Mobile Services. I'd like to inform you of some irregularities on your phone usage this past month. As you may be aware, your phone bill has remained constant and averages $50.00 every month. Recently, however, your records show that you've been making numerous international calls to different countries using your cell phone and as of now your balance stands at $233.25. As a member of our customer protection plan, you will not be responsible for the charges should these calls be a result of phone theft or similar cases. In addition, please be advised that you must notify us before May 1st to report a fraudulent charge. Please call us back at 332-4958 and let us know whether there has been any mistake. Thank you.

試　　題

**95.** What is the message about?
(A) Irregularities in phone usage
(B) A customer protection plan
(C) Special international rates
(D) Customer satisfaction survey

**96.** What does the speaker suggest?
(A) To make international calls
(B) To pay the bill before May 1st
(C) To return his call
(D) To join the customer protection plan

**97.** What is the charge that Mr. Albertson normally pays?
(A) About $33.00
(B) About $50.00
(C) About $200.00
(D) About $233.00

## 中文翻譯

Albertson 先生，您好，我是 Systel 手機服務公司的 Laurence Wilco。我要通知您，上個月您電話使用的一些異常情形。您自己或許知道，您的電話費用長期以來都維持在每個月平均 50 美元。不過最近通話紀錄顯示，您用手機撥出很多通越洋電話到國外，所以本月帳單高達 233.25 美元。您是我們客戶保護專案的客戶，萬一這些通話是因為您電話遭竊之類的情形而造成，您毋需負擔這些費用。還有，您務必在 5 月 1 日之前告知我們，以便申報詐欺費用。麻煩您回電 332-4958，讓我們了解有無任何失誤，感謝您！

**試題** **95.** 此段留言是關於何事？ **解 答** **(A)**
(A) 電話使用的異常狀況
(B) 客戶保護專案
(C) 特定的越洋費率
(D) 客戶滿意度調查

**96.** 說話者有何建議？ **解 答** **(C)**
(A) 撥打國際電話
(B) 5 月 1 日之前繳款
(C) 回電
(D) 參加客戶保護專案

**Part 4**

**97.** Albertson 先生平常的費用是多少？ **解 答** **(B)**
(A) 大約 $33.00
(B) 大約 $50.00
(C) 大約 $200.00
(D) 大約 $233.00

**註 解**

| | | | |
|---|---|---|---|
| mobile | n. 行動電話 | inform | v. 通知 |
| irregularity | n. 異常狀況 | usage | n. 使用 |
| aware | a. 知道的 | constant | a. 固定的 |
| record | n. 記錄 | numerous | a. 許多的 |
| international call | 國際電話 | balance | n. 結餘，餘額 |
| stand | v. 位於 | customer protection plan | 客戶保護方案 |
| charge | n. 收費 | result | n. 結果 |
| theft | n. 偷竊 | notify | v. 告知 |
| fraudulent | a. 欺詐的 | | |

**聽力原文** Questions **98** through **100** refer to the following talk.

Good afternoon and welcome to Pleasant Ridge Residence. My name is Tiffany Reese, the General Manager of Collins & Collins Property Management Group and I'll be giving you a brief overview of these facilities. First of all, our recreation center, which is open from 8 a.m. to 10 p.m., includes a reading area, free refreshments and snacks, and a common area equipped with state-of-the-art audio-visual equipment. Across from here, you can see the laundry room and convenience store. The fitness center is open from 6 a.m. to 12 a.m. and comes with a swimming pool, a weight room, and a racket ball court. Now, before we begin this tour, are there any questions you'd like to ask?

**試　　題**

**98.**　What is the talk mainly about?
(A) To sell apartment units
(B) To offer apartment rentals
(C) To describe various facilifies
(D) To discuss a sports program

**99.**　What is the name of the property?
(A) Collins & Collins Property Management Group
(B) Pleasant Ridge Residence
(C) Timothy Reese
(D) Mandy Evans

**100.**　What hours is the fitness center open?
(A) From 8 a.m. to 10 p.m.
(B) 24 hours a day.
(C) From 6 a.m. to 12 a.m.
(D) It will be unavailable until next fall.

中文翻譯

　　各位午安，歡迎來到 Pleasant Ridge Residence。我叫 Tiffany Reese，我是 Collins & Collins 房地產管理集團的總經理，現在要為您簡單介紹這些設備。首先呢，我們的休閒中心開放時間是早上八點到晚上十點。裡面有閱讀區，免費供應的飲料點心，還有設有頂級影音設備的公共區域。從這裡過去，您可以看到洗衣房和便利商店。健身中心是從早上六點開放到晚上十二點，附有游泳池、舉重室以及回力球場。現在，在我們開始參觀之前，不知各位有沒有任何問題？

試題　**98.** 此段談話主題為何？　解　答　**(C)**
(A) 銷售公寓房子
(B) 提供出租公寓
(C) 介紹各項設備
(D) 討論運動節目

**99.** 這棟建築名稱為何？　解　答　**(B)**
(A) Collins & Collins Property Management Group
(B) Pleasant Ridge Residence
(C) Timothy Reese
(D) Mandy Evans

Part
4

**100.** 健身中心何時開放？　解　答　**(C)**
(A) 早上 8 點到晚上 10 點。
(B) 全天 24 小時。
(C) 早上 6 點到晚上 12 點。
(D) 明年秋天才開放。

註　解

| | | | |
|---|---|---|---|
| residence | n. 住所，公館 | general manager | 總經理 |
| property management group | 房地產管理集團 | | |
| brief | a. 簡略的 | overview | n. 概述 |
| facility | n. 設備 | recreation center | 休閒中心 |
| reading area | 閱讀區 | refreshment | n. 飲料，點心 |
| common area | 公共區域 | equip | v. 配備 |
| state-of-the-art | a. 最頂級的 | audio-visual | 影音 |
| laundry room | 洗衣房 | convenience store | 便利商店 |
| fitness center | 健身中心 | weight room | 舉重室 |
| racket ball court | 回力球場 | | |

# Part 5 Incomplete Sentences

## 「句子填空」的特點與對策

### 題型說明

在這個部份共有 40 題，每題都有一個空格。請從每題的四個選項當中，選出最適合的答案，使句子完整。

### 基本對策

**1** 閱讀部份想要全部作完，一定要好好控管時間（Time management），單句填空最好在 20 分鐘內作完。

**2** 為爭取作答時間，可以直接看空格的前後文找答案，不一定要從頭逐字閱讀。

**3** 本部份主要題型分為字彙、文法、習慣用法三大項：

（1）字彙題：

A. 運用字首、字根、字尾的概念來選擇最佳的字彙。

B. 注意功能接近或意思接近，但用法不同的混淆字，如 cease，stop。

C. 注意拼字類似，但意思完全不同的混淆字，如 desert，deserts，dessert。

（2）文法題：

A. 常考詞性，由空格前後文即可辨識應填入字的正確詞性。

B. 動詞時態的考題，要找與時間有關的單字來判斷。

C. 要注意一致性，如主詞、動詞、所有格、單複數等彼此之間的文法關係。

（3）習慣用法：

A. 常考片語中的介詞，以及分別表示時間、地點、位置、方式等不同用法。

B. 多留意慣用語的使用，即字詞搭配，辨識應加原形動詞、動名詞或不定詞等。如 avoid 後面一定用動名詞。

# READING TEST

In the Reading test, you will read a variety of texts and answer several different types of reading comprehension questions. The entire Reading test will last 75 minutes. There are three parts, and directions are given for each part. You are encouraged to answer as many questions as possible within the time allowed.

You must mark your answers on the separate answer sheet. Do not write your answers in the test book.

## Part 5

**Directions:** A word or phrase is missing in each of the sentences below. Four answer choices are given below each sentence. Select the best answer to complete the sentence. Then mark the letter (A), (B), (C), or (D) on your answer sheet.

**101.** With the elections over, the new government could now
_____ its attention toward solving the problem of poverty
and unemployment.

(A) alter

(B) turn

(C) change

(D) transform

**102.** It just made Ms. Tracy _____ about the way that nobody
listened to her opinions during the meeting.

(A) be angry

(B) angry

(C) angered

(D) angrily

---

中文翻譯

解 答 **(B)**

**101.** 隨著選舉結束,新政府現在可以將它的注意
力,轉向解決貧窮和失業問題。

(A) 改變

(B) 轉向

(C) 變化

(D) 徹底改造

註 解

turn ;「轉移注意力」應當用
turn attention,故正答是 (B)。

· alter      v. 更動,改變
· transform   v. 徹底改造
· election     n. 選舉
· government   n. 政府
· solve       v. 解決
· unemployment
   n. 失業 ( 人口 )

Part

**5**

中文翻譯

解 答 **(B)**

**102.** 會議中,沒有人聽 Tracy 小姐的意見,讓她
很生氣。

(A) 生氣的

(B) 生氣的

(C) 生氣

(D) 生氣地

註 解

make +受詞+補語,補語用
形容詞;補語若是動詞的話,
則用動詞原形。本題 angry
是形容詞,angered 是動詞
過去式或過去分詞,angrily
是副詞,故答案為 (B)。

**103.** The chemical factory has been fined heavily by the Environmental Bureau for _____ a nearby lake.

- (A) polluting
- (B) soiling
- (C) smudging
- (D) staining

**104.** If their company cut _____ on several construction projects, they might increase their profits by 20 percent.

- (A) edges
- (B) sides
- (C) corners
- (D) ends

---

中文翻譯

**103.** 這家化工廠被環保局處以高額罰款，因為它污染了附近的湖泊。
- (A) 污染
- (B) 弄髒
- (C) 弄髒
- (D) 沾污

解　答　**(A)**

註　解

polluting；pollute v. 污染 ，符合句意。
- fine　　　v. 處以罰金
- bureau
　n.（政府機構的）局，處
- soil　　　v. 弄污，弄髒
- smudge　v. 弄髒，留下污跡
- stain　　v. 沾污，染污

解　答　**(C)**

中文翻譯

**104.** 如果他們公司減少幾項建造計劃案的開銷，就可能增加 20% 的利潤。
- (A) 邊緣
- (B) 面，邊
- (C) 角落
- (D) 末端

註　解

corners；cut corners（為節省時間、金錢或精力而）草草行事
- edge　　　　n. 邊，邊緣
- end　　　　n. 端，末端
- construction　n. 建設，建造
- project　　　n. 計畫；企劃案
- increase　　v. 增加
- profit　　　n. 收益，利潤
- percent　　n. 百分比

**105.** Her picky boss used to scold her _____ coming to work late, even if it was only three minutes.

(A) in

(B) to

(C) for

(D) of

**106.** The Mayor felt _____ sympathy for the victims of the fire disaster, but there was nothing more he could do to help.

(A) deep

(B) big

(C) hard

(D) full

---

中文翻譯

解　答 **(C)**

**105.** 愛挑剔的老闆以前常責備她上班遲到，即使只是遲到三分鐘。

(A) in

(B) to

(C) for

(D) of

註　解

scold someone for sth. 為…而責備某人
· used to ...　以前常…
· picky　　a. 愛挑剔的，吹毛求疵的
· even if = no matter if 即使，縱然

Part

**5**

中文翻譯

解　答 **(A)**

**106.** 市長對火災的受害者深表同情，但他卻幫不上忙。

(A) 強烈的

(B) 大的

(C) 無情的

(D) 充滿的

註　解

· full　a. 完全的，充滿的
· hard　a. 費心的，無情的
· mayor　n. 市長，鎮長
· victim　n. 受害者，犧牲者
· disaster n. 災難；災害

**107.** We must have all of our financial records in order because we could expect an _____ from the tax office anytime.

(A) coverage

(B) inspecting

(C) checklist

(D) inquisition

**108.** We were discouraged when we realized how _____ the ruined palace was.

(A) quiet

(B) solitary

(C) desolate

(D) lonesome

---

中文翻譯

**107.** 我們必須要依序整理所有的財務紀錄，因為稅務局隨時都可能會來調查。

(A) 新聞報導

(B) 檢查，檢驗

(C) 清單，一覽表

(D) （政治上、宗教上）偵查，調查

解 答 **(B)**

註 解

inspecting 檢查，檢驗，是 inspect 的現在分詞、動名詞。
- financial a. 財務的
- record n. 紀錄，記載
- in order
  合乎程序的，按照順序

---

中文翻譯

**108.** 當我們知道這破敗不堪的大廈是多麼荒涼時，我們很洩氣。

(A) 平靜的

(B) 單一的

(C) 荒涼的

(D) 孤單的

解 答 **(C)**

註 解

破敗不堪的大廈可用 desolate （荒涼的，無人居住的）來形容。
- solitary a. 孤獨的，唯一的
- desolate a. 荒涼的，
  無人居住的
- lonesome a. 孤單的，孤寂的
- ruined a. 破敗的
- palace n. 大廈；皇宮

**109.** When Alison entered her office, she found the window open and something _____.

   (A) to steal

   (B) stolen

   (C) stealing

   (D) steal

**110.** Perhaps the most common and convenient form of entertainment and _____ outside the home is going to the movies.

   (A) relax

   (B) relaxed

   (C) relaxing

   (D) relaxation

---

中文翻譯

解　答 **(B)**

**109.** 當 Alison 進到辦公室，她發現窗戶是開著的，有某些東西被偷了。

   (A) 偷　（不定詞）

   (B) 被偷（過去分詞）

   (C) 偷　（現在分詞）

   (D) 偷　（原形動詞）

註　解

find + O. + adj.，open 和 stolen 都是形容詞。因為物品遭竊，故選用被動語態的過去分詞 stolen。

Part

**5**

中文翻譯

解　答 **(D)**

**110.** 或許最普遍也最方便的戶外休閒、娛樂的方式，就是看電影。

   (A) 休息（動詞）

   (B) 休息（過去式；過去分詞）

   (C) 休息（現在分詞）

   (D) 休息（名詞）

註　解

動詞 relax 的名詞是 relaxation，此處應該用名詞形容。

· convenient　　a. 近便的

· entertainment　n. 娛樂

· relaxed　　　a. 輕鬆的

· relaxing　　　a. 使人懶洋洋的

· relaxation　　n. 消遣，娛樂

**111.** Before becoming president in 2007, he _____ as deputy manager.

    (A) has served

    (B) was served

    (C) would serve

    (D) served

**112.** Although both of them were trying to take the _____ of the sales meeting, John forgot to attend it.

    (A) minutes

    (B) notices

    (C) notes

    (D) memoirs

---

中文翻譯　　　　　　　　　　　　解　答　**(D)**

**111.** 在 2007 年成為總經理之前,他擔任副理。

    (A) 一直任職

    (B) 被供應

    (C) 可能任職

    (D) 任職

註　解

時間的先後關係很明確的話,前後兩個子句用連接詞 (after, before, when, till, as soon as) 連接時,可以用過去式代替過去完成式,故 served 是正答。had served 亦可。
・serve　v. 任職於;為…工作
・deputy　n. 副手;代理人

中文翻譯　　　　　　　　　　　　解　答　**(A)**

**112.** 雖然他們兩人打算在業務會議中做會議記錄,可是 John 卻忘了去參加。

    (A) 記錄

    (B) 告示

    (C) 筆記

    (D) 回憶錄

註　解

minutes ; take the minutes 做會議紀錄。

**113.** In business, where knowledge is power, anyone _____ information in advance is in a position to gain advantage from it.
(A) gets
(B) who gets
(C) who does he get
(D) if he gets

**114.** Elgin General Practice _____ in this district for more than decades.
(A) has lain
(B) has laid
(C) laid
(D) lie

---

中文翻譯

解　答 **(B)**

**113.** 在商界，知識就是力量，任何人率先獲得資訊就是處於優勢。
(A) 獲得
(B) 他獲得
(C) 他獲得？
(D) 若他獲得

註　解
· in advance　預先，提前
· advantage　n. 有利條件，優勢

Part
**5**

中文翻譯

解　答 **(A)**

**114.** Elgin 綜合診所在這地區已經超過幾十年了。
(A) 位於 (lain 為 lie 之過去分詞 )
(B) 放置 (laid 為 lay 之過去分詞 )
(C) 放置 (laid 為 lay 之過去式 )
(D) 平躺，位於 ( 原形動詞 )

註　解
has lain；lie 位於 (lain 為 lie 之過去分詞 )
· general practice 綜合診所
· decade　　　n. 十年

**115.** The chief executive officer always delivers a speech for a
_____ purpose at the meeting every morning.
(A) speculative
(B) prolific
(C) concrete
(D) specific

**116.** Simon was surprised to hear that half of the computer parts
were _____ and had to be replaced.
(A) definite
(B) inefficient
(C) defective
(D) punctual

---

中文翻譯　　　　　　　　　　　　解　答　**(D)**

**115.** 執行長總是在每天早上的會議中，針對
特定的目標發表言論。
(A) 猜測性的，投機性的
(B) 豐富的
(C) 具體的
(D) 特定的

註　解

specific 特定的。符合句意。
· deliver a speech /lecture/
an address
發表演說 / 正式談話
· purpose　n. 目標，目的

中文翻譯　　　　　　　　　　　　解　答　**(C)**

**116.** Simon 得知半數的電腦零件有瑕疵，必
須更換，頗感訝異。
(A) 明確的，確實的
(B) 效率低的
(C) 有瑕疵的，有毛病的
(D) 準時的，按時的

註　解

defective 有瑕疵的，有毛病
的。符合句意。
· parts　n. 零件
· replace　v. 更換

**117.** In _____ with the company regulations, his pay was cut ten percent because of his gross negligence.

(A) accord

(B) accordance

(C) accordingly

(D) account

**118.** Joe tried to _____ up his schedule to go to Korea for a business trip, but he was tied up with the union meeting.

(A) put

(B) show

(C) free

(D) clean

---

中文翻譯　　　　　　　　　　　　　　　　　解　答　**(B)**

**117.** 按照公司規定，他因為重大過失而遭減薪10%。

(A) 符合，一致

(B) 依照，按照

(C) 因此，相應地

(D) 報導，敘述

註　解

accordance；此處要用名詞，構成片語 in accordance with ... 依照，依據。
· regulation　n. 規定
· gross negligence 重大過失

Part **5**

中文翻譯　　　　　　　　　　　　　　　　　解　答　**(C)**

**118.** Joe 試圖騰出時間去韓國出差，卻因工會的會議而動彈不得。

(A) put up　擺放

(B) show up 顯示

(C) free up　騰出

(D) clean up 清理

註　解

free；free up 省下，騰出
· business trip　n. 出差
· be tied up
　動彈不得，無法分身

**119.** Only a few people could stand the hard and _____ rules and regulations of the company, and most of us ended up quitting.
(A) slim
(B) cold
(C) narrow
(D) fast

**120.** The research and development team was up _____ a blank wall when many unexpected troubles were found in their plan.
(A) upon
(B) against
(C) on
(D) to

---

中文翻譯

**119.** 只有少數人能忍受公司嚴厲死板的規章制度，我們大部份人最後都辭職了。
(A) 微小的
(B) 冷的
(C) 狹窄的
(D) 牢固的，緊緊的

解　答 **(D)**

註　解
fast  a. 牢固的，緊緊的
・rules and regulations
　規則，規章制度
・end up +Ving 最後⋯

中文翻譯

**120.** 研發團隊發現計劃中有許多沒預料到的難題時，感到不知所措。
(A) 在⋯上
(B) 面臨
(C) 在⋯上
(D) 朝向

解　答 **(B)**

註　解
against ; be up against
面臨 ( 困境 )
・blank wall 茫然，一片空白

**121.** The famous detective novelist was caught in the _____ of shoplifting at a shopping plaza in New York.

(A) way

(B) moment

(C) scene

(D) act

**122.** As management proposed a ten-percent downsizing, the head of the trade union continued to _____ tooth and nail.

(A) comment

(B) deny

(C) conflict

(D) negotiate

---

中文翻譯

解　答 (D)

**121.** 這位知名的偵探小說作家在紐約的一家購物中心行竊時，當場被逮捕。

(A) 方式

(B) 一剎那

(C) 場面

(D) 行動

註　解

act 行動。符合句意。
· detective　a. 偵探的
· shoplift　v. 順手牽羊，行竊

Part

**5**

中文翻譯

解　答 (D)

**122.** 管理階層提出要裁員百分之十，工會領導人竭盡全力繼續協商。

(A) 評論

(B) 否認

(C) 衝突

(D) 協商

註　解

negotiate　協商，談判。符合句意。
· downsize
　v. 縮編，縮小規模
· trade union　工會
· tooth and nail　竭盡全力地

**123.** Michael was _____ with a new portfolio project, but he felt it tough to complete the job by himself.

(A) entrusted

(B) integrated

(C) strengthened

(D) enthralled

**124.** There are many cases in which small-sized manufacturers make cutbacks in production because of an operating funds _____.

(A) short

(B) shorten

(C) shortage

(D) shortly

---

中 文 翻 譯

解　　答 **(A)**

**123.** Michael 受委託作一項新的投資組合的企劃案，但他覺得那是一件很難獨力完成的工作。

(A) 委託

(B) 使結合，合併

(C) 增強實力

(D) 吸引

註　　解

entrusted；entrust 委託
・integrate v. 使融入，使結合
・portfolio n. 投資組合，系列

中 文 翻 譯

解　　答 **(C)**

**124.** 小型製造廠商常因為營運資金短缺，而削減產量。

(A) 短的　　　（形容詞）

(B) 縮短　　　（動詞）

(C) 短缺　　　（名詞）

(D) 很快，不久（副詞）

註　　解

shortage 短缺，缺乏
・cutback n. 削減，減少
・operating funds 營運資金

**125.** It's amazing how many people think about their workplace from a social _____.
(A) skill
(B) perspective
(C) contact
(D) call

**126.** If your contribution doesn't far outweigh your expense, sooner or later management will consider _____ you.
(A) demote
(B) to demote
(C) demoting
(D) demoted

---

中文翻譯

**125.** 許多人以社交的角度看待他們的工作場所，真令人詫異！
(A) 技巧，能力
(B) 眼光，角度
(C) 接觸
(D) 拜訪

解答 **(B)**

註解
perspective 角度，眼光
・contact n. 接觸
・amazing
　a. 令人吃驚的，驚人的

Part **5**

中文翻譯

**126.** 假使你的貢獻沒辦法遠超過你的薪水，高層主管遲早會將你降職。
(A) 降職（動詞原形）
(B) 降職（不定詞片語）
(C) 降職（動名詞）
(D) 降職（過去分詞）

解答 **(C)**

註解
demoting ; demote 降職，降級 ; consider + Ving
・contribution n. 貢獻，捐助
・outweigh v. 價值上超過

**127.** Sam Walton would enjoy the mental exercise of figuring out how to improve Wal-Mart's _____ network.
(A) distributing
(B) distributor
(C) distribution
(D) distributed

**128.** He would rather be out with the employees doing the real work of _____ than sitting around in meeting in the home office.
(A) purchase
(B) retail
(C) trade
(D) consumption

---

中文翻譯

解 答 **(C)**

**127.** Sam Walton 樂於反覆思考如何改善 Wal-Mart 的配銷網。
(A) 分發，分配
(B) 經銷商，批發商
(C) 配銷，分送
(D) 分配 ( 佈 ) 的

註 解
distribution 配銷，分送。名詞當形容詞用，符合句意。
· mental  a. 思維的，理解的
· figure out  理解，想出

中文翻譯

解 答 **(B)**

**128.** 他寧願出去和真正做零售工作的員工在一起，而不願只坐在總部辦公室開會。
(A) 採購
(B) 零售
(C) 交易
(D) 消耗

註 解
retail 零售。合乎句意。
· home office
  居家辦公室，總部辦公室

**129.** It is quite _____ to develop and market your own private-label line of products and services.

    (A) available

    (B) easygoing

    (C) feasible

    (D) reliable

**130.** As network effects _____, the brand or company can enjoy explosive growth.

    (A) catch on

    (B) kick in

    (C) set in

    (D) turn in

---

中文翻譯

解　答 **(C)**

**129.** 開發且推出自有品牌的產品和服務，是相當可行的。

    (A) 可獲得的

    (B) 隨和的

    (C) 可行的，可能的

    (D) 可靠的

註　解

feasible 可行的，可能的。符合句意。

· easygoing　a. 隨和的

· private-label　自有品牌

Part **5**

中文翻譯

解　答 **(B)**

**130.** 當網路效果奏效時，品牌或公司就能享有爆炸性的成長。

    (A) 流行，風行

    (B) 起作用，奏效

    (C) 盛行，來臨

    (D) 產生，交給

註　解

kick in　起作用，奏效

· brand　　n. 品牌

· explosive　a. 爆炸性的

**131.** Blogs are now considered to be a _____ way for companies to get their messages and ideas out into the marketplace.

    (A) reasonable

    (B) legitimate

    (C) sensible

    (D) unlawful

**132.** Although the sales promotion plan was _____ made, Cynthia was not able to conduct the project efficiently.

    (A) directly

    (B) conclusively

    (C) trivially

    (D) minutely

---

**中文翻譯**

**131.** 部落格是目前許多公司視為對市場發送訊息與觀念的正常管道。

    (A) 合理的，理智的

    (B) 正常的，合法的

    (C) 合理的，明智的

    (D) 非法的

**解　答 (B)**

**註　解**

legitimate 正常的，合法的。符合句意。

· sensible　a. 合乎實際的

· blog　n. 部落格，網誌

**中文翻譯**

**132.** 雖然這項推銷計畫很周密，但 Cynthia 仍無法有效率地進行這個方案。

    (A) 直接地

    (B) 毫無疑問地，有說服力的

    (C) 瑣碎地

    (D) 周密地，仔細地

**解　答 (D)**

**註　解**

minutely 周密地，仔細地。合乎句意。

· conduct　v.　進行

· efficiently　adv. 效率高地

**133.** Morgan is a competent mechanical engineer who is really on
_____ of his job.
(A) basis
(B) top
(C) grip
(D) grasp

**134.** The Secretary of the Economy said on the TV program that
the end of the depression was already in _____.
(A) short
(B) sight
(C) time
(D) case

---

中文翻譯

解　答 **(B)**

**133.** Morgan 是一位能確實掌握工作的稱職的機
械工程師。
(A) 根據，基礎
(B) 控制著…
(C) 控制，緊握
(D) 理解力

註　解
top；on top of 對…完全掌
握
・ competent
　 a. 能幹的，能勝任的
・ mechanical　a. 機械的

Part
**5**

中文翻譯

解　答 **(B)**

**134.** 經濟部長在電視節目上說：經濟不景氣已經
快結束了。
(A) in short 簡單地說
(B) in sight 在即，看得見
(C) in time 及時
(D) in case 如果，也許

註　解
sight；in sight 在即，看得
見，符合句意。
・ secretary　n. 部長，秘書
・ depression
　 n. 蕭條，不景氣

**135.** This is the empty lot which the skyscraper is to be _____ in by the conglomerate.

   (A) blocked

   (B) reinforced

   (C) destroyed

   (D) constructed

**136.** Patrick, our consultant, subscribes _____ several economic and financial magazines.

   (A) in

   (B) on

   (C) to

   (D) for

---

中文翻譯　　　　　　　　　　　　解　答 **(D)**

**135.** 這塊空地就是企業集團即將建築摩天大樓的地方。

   (A) 擋住，阻塞

   (B) 補強，加固

   (C) 摧毀，破壞

   (D) 建造，建築

註　解

constructed；construct 建築，建造

・lot　　　　　　n. (特定用途)小塊土地

・skyscraper　　n. 摩天樓

・conglomerate　n. 企業集團

中文翻譯　　　　　　　　　　　　解　答 **(C)**

**136.** 我們的顧問 Patrick，訂閱好幾種財經雜誌。

   (A) in

   (B) on

   (C) to

   (D) for

註　解

to；subscribe to sth. 訂閱…

・consultant　n. 顧問

・subscribe　　v. 訂閱，訂購

**137.** The management urged her to think _____ before quitting, but that didn't change her mind.
(A) all
(B) twice
(C) back
(D) secondly

**138.** Though Donna's promotion campaign plan was rejected twice by her boss, she tried _____ third time.
(A) the
(B) a
(C) an
(D) to

---

中文翻譯　　　　　　　　　　　　　解　答　**(B)**

**137.** 管理階層力勸她在辭職前再三考慮，但仍無法改變她的心意。
(A) 全部
(B) 兩次
(C) think back 回想
(D) 其次

註　解

twice；think twice 再三考慮
· management  n. 管理階層
· urge　　　　v. 力勸，催促

Part
**5**

中文翻譯　　　　　　　　　　　　　解　答　**(B)**

**138.** 雖然 Donna 的促銷活動計劃，被她老闆駁回了兩次，她又試了第三次。
(A) the
(B) a
(C) an
(D) to

註　解

· promotion campaign
　促銷活動
· reject　　v. 駁回，否決

**139.** The Lego Group started _____ all of its help desk calls received as entries on a customer support website.

(A) posting

(B) posted

(C) be posted

(D) post

**140.** The company has no designers, but uses designs and ideas _____ by customers for its new products .

(A) ordered

(B) submitted

(C) prescribed

(D) appreciated

---

**中文翻譯**

**139.** 樂高集團開始把客服部門接到的詢問電話，逐項公佈在顧客支援網站上。

(A) 張貼（動名詞）

(B) 張貼（過去分詞）

(C) 張貼（被動式）

(D) 張貼（現在式）

**解　答** **(A)**

**註　解**

posting；post 張貼，公告
· help desk
　客服部門，服務台
· entry　　　　n. 項目
· support website 支援網站

**中文翻譯**

**140.** 這家公司並沒有設計師，而是利用顧客提供的設計和構想來生產新產品。

(A) 下訂單的

(B) 提供的

(C) 開處方的

(D) 欣賞的

**解　答** **(B)**

**註　解**

submitted 提供的。符合句意。
· prescribe  v. 開處方
· designer  n. 設計師

# Part 6 Text Completion

## 「短文克漏字」的特點與對策

## 題型說明

　　此部份共有三或四篇短文，每篇短文都有四或三個空格，共有 12 題。每題都有四個選項，請選出最適合的答案，使整篇文章完整。

## 基本對策

**1** 此部份可視為短文閱讀中的句子填空，答題策略亦與 Part 4 相同，作答時間最好不超過 10 分鐘。

**2** 先看空格前後文，不須看完全文，以爭取作答時間。

**3** 注意連接詞，以正確掌握句意。

Questions **141-144** refer to the following article.

The core of your online marketing should be one simple and solid credo: you are _____ you publish on the Web. Therefore,

**141.** (A) what
(B) which
(C) whatever
(D) whichever

the key to your success will be to place great online content that will generate the visitor's interest and motivate him to make a deal withyou. When a visitor wants to purchase anything, he usually turns to the Web to do some comparison shopping. This is the _____ of truth.

**142.** (A) time
(B) schedule
(C) moment
(D) timing

When he browses among your Website, is he attracted by it or does he click away to the next one _____ by a search engine?

**143.** (A) suggesting
(B) suggested
(C) to suggest
(D) has suggested

To attract a lot of attention, you need to have good content on your Website and a way for first-time visitors to quickly find what they need. Everything you do should be aimed directly at getting people into moving _____ buying, subscribing or joining you as members.

**144.** (A) over
(B) along
(C) towards
(D) on

中文翻譯

　　網路行銷的核心應該是單純而實在的信條：你在網路所公佈的，就代表了你。因此成功的關鍵就是發佈引起點閱者興趣、促使他和你交易的極佳網路內容。當點閱者要購買東西時，通常會上網貨比三家。這是關鍵時刻！當他瀏覽你的網站時，是會被它所吸引？或者離開你的頁面，到搜尋引擎建議的下一個網站？要吸引眾多的注意，你必須在網站呈現極佳的內容，同時要有辦法讓首次點閱者迅速找到他們所需要的東西。你做的每一件事情，都應該直接針對讓人上門購物、訂閱，或成為你的會員。

**141.** (A) what
(B) which
(C) whatever
(D) whichever

解答 **(A)**

**142.** (A) time
(B) schedule
(C) moment
(D) timing

解答 **(C)**

**143.** (A) suggesting
(B) suggested
(C) to suggest
(D) has suggested

解答 **(B)**

**144.** (A) over
(B) along
(C) towards
(D) on

解答 **(C)**

註　解

| | | | |
|---|---|---|---|
| · core | n. 核心 | · online marketing | 網路行銷 |
| · solid | adv. 積極地 | · credo = creed | n. 信條 |
| · publish | n. 發表，公佈 | · generate | v. 引發，引起 |
| · motivate | v. 促使，激起 | · comparison | n. 比較 |
| · the moment of truth | 關鍵時刻，重要關頭 | · browse | v. 瀏覽 |
| · attract | v. 吸引 | · click | v. （電腦）點選 |
| · search engine | （電腦）搜尋引擎 | · subscribe | v. 訂閱，訂購 |

Part

6

Questions **145-148** refer to the following report.

With more time on their hands and more money in their wallets than ever before, European are trying to enrich their lives in their spare time. It's clear that they want something _____ their jobs and family duties.

**145.** (A) from
(B) on
(C) between
(D) beyond

The growth of education has encouraged people to take _____ new

**146.** (A) over
(B) up
(C) in
(D) out

interests—from making wooden chair to studying computer technology— to expand their lives in their own ways and on their own time. Interest in cultural events is increasing, and a large number of Europeans want to create something on their own. They don't want to watch other _____

**147.** (A) prudent
(B) accredited
(C) talented
(D) congenial

artists. For a close look at what many are _____ in leisure

**148.** (A) accomplishment
(B) accomplish
(C) accomplishing
(D) accomplished

hours and how this has changed their lives, *Business Magazine Monthly* interviewed men and women from British to Germany.

# TEXT COMPLETION

　　比起以前，現在的歐洲人手邊有更多的時間，皮夾裡也有更多的金錢，這讓他們在閒暇時，試著去充實他們的生活。很顯然地，他們所想要的是超越工作和家庭責任的某些東西。教育的成長一直鼓勵人們去培養新的興趣——從做木椅到學習電腦科技——以他們自己的方式和用他們自己的時間，拓展他們的生活。對人文活動的興趣逐漸提升，很多歐洲人想要自己創造東西，他們不要只是觀看其他有天份的藝術家。為了要仔細觀察許多人在閒暇時，究竟完成了什麼，以及這又如何改變了他們的生活，《商業雜誌月刊》從英國到德國，訪問了多位男性與女性。

**145.** (A) from　　　　　　　　　　　　　解 答 **(D)**
(B) on
(C) between
(D) beyond

**146.** (A) over　　　　　　　　　　　　　解 答 **(B)**
(B) up
(C) in
(D) out

**147.** (A) prudent　　　　　　　　　　　　解 答 **(C)**
(B) accredited
(C) talented
(D) congenial

**148.** (A) accomplishment　　　　　　　　　解 答 **(D)**
(B) accomplish
(C) accomplishing
(D) accomplished

註　解

| | | | |
|---|---|---|---|
| · wallet | n. 錢包，皮夾 | · spare | a. 空閒的，多餘的 |
| · take over | 接管，接手 | · take up | 對…產生興趣，從事… |
| · take in | 收養，收容，包括 | · take out | 帶…出去，獲得 |
| · interest | n. 興趣 | · technology | n. 科技 |
| · prudent | a. 明智的，慎重的 | · accredited | a. 得到授權的 |
| · talented | a. 有天份的 | · congenial | a. 令人舒適愉快的 |
| · leisure | n. 閒暇 | · accomplish | v. 完成，取得成功 |

Part

6

Questions **149-152** refer to the following certificate.

## Warranty for the OK2008 Stereo

❖ This product is guaranteed _____ any defects in parts

**149.** (A) for
(B) by
(C) to
(D) against

or workmanship for 1 year past the purchase date. This warranty only applies to manufacturer defects, and does not apply to any problems the customer may encounter _____ abuse, severe environments or accidents.

**150.** (A) according to
(B) supposing
(C) due to
(D) regarding

❖ If the product has been found to be defective, the customer should bring the product with this warranty certificate as well as receipt of purchase to the place of purchase. The defective product will be sent for repair back to the manufacturer at the company's _____. The product without the

**151.** (A) expense
(B) perk
(C) expenditure
(D) account

company's approval will not be replaced.

❖ In the case that damage is the customer's fault, no repair or replacement will be done for free. If the damaged product is brought back with this warranty, repair can be done at a

_____.

**152.** (A) rebate
(B) refund
(C) discount
(D) reimburse

中文翻譯

## OK2008 音響保證書

❖ 本產品自購買日起一年內為保固期，保固內容包括任何零件或製造上的瑕疵。保固僅限於原廠製造之瑕疵，不含任何因顧客使用不當、置於惡劣環境或意外造成之損害。

❖ 如發現產品有瑕疵，顧客須攜帶本產品暨保證書，連同購買收據，到原購買處辦理。 有瑕疵之產品將會送回原廠維修，並由本公司付費。未經本公司同意，不得更換商品。

❖ 如產品損害是顧客造成，則須自費維修或換貨。損害之產品和保證書一併送回，將提供維修折扣優惠。

**149.** (A) for
(B) by
(C) to
(D) against

解答 **(D)**

**150.** (A) according to
(B) supposing
(C) due to
(D) regarding

解答 **(C)**

**151.** (A) expense
(B) perk
(C) expenditure
(D) account

解答 **(A)**

**152.** (A) rebate
(B) refund
(C) discount
(D) reimburse

解答 **(C)**

註 解

| | | | |
|---|---|---|---|
| · warranty | n. ( 商品 ) 保證書 | · guarantee | v. 保證 |
| · defect | n. 缺點，瑕疵 | · parts | n. 零件 |
| · apply | v. 適用，應用 | · manufacturer | n. 製造商，廠商 |
| · encounter | v. 發現，偶遇 | · due to | 由於 |
| · abuse | n. 濫用，虐待 | · severe | a. 惡劣的，嚴重的 |
| · environment | n. 環境 | · defective | a. 有缺點 ( 毛病 ) 的 |
| · certificate | n. 證明，證書 | · receipt | n. 收據 |
| · replace | v. 更換，替換 | · approval | n. 贊同，認可 |
| · damage | n. 損害，損傷 | | |

Part

6

# Part 7 Reading Comprehension

## 「文章閱讀」的特點與對策

**Part 7**
**Directions:** In this part you will read a selection of texts, such as magazine and newspaper articles, letters, and advertisements. Each text is followed by several questions. Select the best answer for each question and mark the letter (A), (B), (C), or (D) on your answer sheet.

### 題型說明

　　本部份共有 48 題，包含數篇不同題材的文章，每篇文章對應幾道試題，每道試題都有四個選項，請選出最適當的答案。單篇閱讀測驗有 28 題，共 8 到 10 篇文章，每篇出 2 到 4 題。雙篇閱讀測驗有 4 組，每組 2 篇文章、5 道題目，共 20 題。

### 基本對策

**1** 務必保留充裕的時間作答（約 45 分鐘），採略讀（skimming）而非精讀。先看標題句，了解主旨，不須理會生字。

**2** 可先快速瀏覽題目，再從文中找答案。不妨先作簡單的題目，覺得困難的題目則運用「刪去法」，也請勿花太多時間，免得因小失大。

**3** 文章類型包括：職場信函、公告、廣告、書報文章、圖表等，平常要多熟悉信件格式、職場訊息等。

**4** 題目類型可分為主旨題與細節題。標題和每段的第一句很重要，往往就是主旨題的線索。

**5** 注意文章中粗黑體、斜體、特別大或小的字體、通常是細節題的出題來源。

Questions **153-154** refer to the following poster.

Classic creation of an American style Italian dinnerhouse with deco of New York, Chicago in 1920's and an open exhibition kitchen.

- Specializing in grand platters of pasta, chicken, prime steak and fresh seafood with reasonable prices.

- Live music nightly 9:00-12:00 featuring the best jazz in city.

- Open for lunch, afternoon tea, dinner, and late night snack.

- A perfect place for any and every kind of party.

**153.** What are people NOT served with in this restaurant ?
(A) music performance
(B) steak and chicken
(C) fastfood
(D) spaghetti

**154.** Which is true for the style of this restaurant's decoration?
(A) It is modern.
(B) It is traditional.
(C) It is odd.
(D) It is fashionable.

中文翻譯

**155.** 此優惠方案以何人為對象？　　　　　　解　答　**(D)**
    (A) 準時繳款的人
    (B) 填好附件表格的人
    (C) 長期使用信用卡的人
    (D) 有 PBA 愛心信用卡的人

**156.** 關於此方案，何者不正確？　　　　　　解　答　**(A)**
    (A) 個人到海外旅行可享低價。
    (B) 2012 年的年費免繳。
    (C) 全國的機票以較低價提供。
    (D) 家人辦附卡免費。

註　解

| | | | |
|---|---|---|---|
| ·rating | n. 等級，級別 | ·qualify | v.（使）取得資格 |
| ·status | n. 狀況，地位 | ·affinity card | 愛心信用卡 |
| ·annual | a. 每年的 | ·resort | n. 度假村 |
| ·airfare | n. 機票費用（價） | ·additional | a. 額外的，附加的 |

Part

**7**

## Questions **157-159** refer to the following memo.

To: All members of the Sales Department
Re: Regional Manager Slot

I have submitted the names listed below to president Morgan Nichol as candidates for promotion to the position of Regional Manager in Charge of Regional Sales. I try to fill the executive position by promotion from within.

Both of them have good credentials for the senior manager slot. They have performed brilliantly at the top level in the Sales Department and have demonstrated persistence and innovation in their endeavors. Their nominations were based on their outstanding performance and ability to coordinate the processing of corporate documents. Their performance has benefited the entire sales team because they are always willing to share their methods and ideas with all team members. They also have served this company for more than ten years. While only one of the nominees can assume the position, both of them would make excellent regional manager.

Therefore, it is my honor and privilege to nominate without reservation the following two names to be our next Regional Manager in Charge of Regional Sales: Vincent Sydool and Gail Dony.

I am sure that one of them will receive the promotion and achieve what he or she is capable of. He or she will do an outstanding job, that's for sure.

Vice-president

問題 157-159 請參考以下的文件。

收件人：業務部全體人員
主　旨：區經理職位

　　我已提出下列名單，呈交總經理 Morgan Nichol，以作為晉升區經理職位候選人，負責區域業務。我要設法提拔內部員工擔任高階主管。

　　這兩位都有極佳的資歷，適任高級經理的職位。他們在業務部表現相當傑出，同時一直努力展現一貫的堅持與創新。提名他們是基於他們傑出的表現以及處理公司文書的協調能力。他們的績效嘉惠了整個業務團隊，因為他們總是願意和所有團隊成員，分享他們的方法和構想。兩個人也已經在這家公司服務超過了十年。雖然僅有一位提名人能獲得晉陞，但是他們兩位都能擔任優秀的區經理。

　　因此，我很高興有這個榮幸，毫無保留地提名以下兩位擔任下一任區經理，負責區域業務：Vincent Sydool 和 Gail Dony。我相信他們其中一位將獲得升遷，並發揮自己的能力，也必然表現出色。

副總經理

Darren Hart

**157.** What is the purpose of this memo?
(A) To make a sales presentation
(B) To promote some hard workers
(C) To congratulate two salespeople
(D) To nominate two people

**158.** Who will make the final decision on promotion?
(A) The sales team members
(B) Vice-president Darren Hart
(C) President Morgan Nichol
(D) Vincent Sydool and Gail Dony

**159.** Why were Vincent and Gail nominated?
(A) They had been at their former position for ten years.
(B) They have worked for the company for many years.
(C) They have done a good job.
(D) The company wanted to take a chance on a newcomer.

**157.** 此文件的目的為何？　　　　　　　　　　解　答　**(D)**
(A) 作業務報告
(B) 提拔一些認真的員工
(C) 恭賀兩位業務人員
(D) 提名兩個人

**158.** 誰將對升遷問題作最後決定？　　　　　　解　答　**(C)**
(A) 業務團隊成員
(B) 副總經理 Darren Hart
(C) 總經理 Morgan Nichol
(D) Vincent Sydool 和 Gail Dony

**159.** Vincent 和 Gail 為何被提名？　　　　　　解　答　**(C)**
(A) 他們已在先前的職位待了十年。
(B) 他們已在公司工作了很多年。
(C) 他們一直表現很好。
(D) 公司要給新人機會。

註　解

| | | | |
|---|---|---|---|
| · solt | n. 職位，位置 | · submit | v. 提交，呈送 |
| · candidate | n. 候選人 | · executive | n. 高階層主管 |
| · credentials | n. 資歷，證書 | · senior | a. 高級的，年長的 |
| · demonstrate | v. 證明，提示 | · persistence | n. 持久，堅持 |
| · innovation | n. 創新，新觀念 | · endeavor | n. 努力，盡力 |
| · nomination | n. 提名，指名 | · outstanding | a. 傑出的 |
| · coordinate | v. 協調 | · corporate | a. 公司的 |
| · nominee | n. 被提名人 | · privilege | n. 榮幸，特權 |
| · former | a. 先前的，前任的 | · newcomer | n. 新來的，新手 |

Part

**7**

Questions **160-162** refer to the following notice.

# NOTICE

★ Please be extremely careful with fire.

★ In the interest of safety, firearms are prohibited.

★ Motor vehicles, including motorcycles, are restricted to vehicle roads and parking areas.

★ Please keep to your campsite. Great damage can be done to the park by careless vehicle parking or tent or trailer location.

★ Please don't damage or remove any flowers, shrubs, trees, mosses and rocks.

★ You will need an angling license if you plan to fish.

★ Help prevent disruption of salmon spawning by keeping pets out of the water, and keep your pet on leash and under control at all times.

★ Please don't litter. The park's lakes and streams are sources of drinking water. Even biodegradable soaps will pollute the water, so will food scraps, fish entrails and dirty plates. Help protect the delicate balance of the water system by washing yourselves, your clothes and your dishes at least 30 meters from lakes or streams and please don't clean fish in them. Preferably use the ocean for all your washing. Please be discreet about the disposal of human waste. Dig a small hole at least 30 meters away from campsites and water sources and cover it after use. Please use toilet facilities whereprovidedand pack out or burn all toilet paper and feminine products.

中文翻譯

問題 160-162 請參考以下的告示。

# 公 告

★ 請特別小心火燭。

★ 為了安全起見,禁止攜帶槍械。

★ 機動車輛(包括機車)限於道路及停車區域行駛。

★ 請在自己的露營區活動。隨意停放車輛、架設帳篷或安置拖車,
均將對公園造成莫大的損害。

★ 請勿破壞或拔除任何花卉、灌木、樹木、苔蘚和石塊。

★ 要釣魚者需要釣魚許可證。

★ 請勿讓寵物靠近水面,繫住並隨時看管,以免鮭魚產卵受到干擾。

★ 請勿亂丟垃圾!公園內的湖泊和河川,都是飲用水的來源。即使是
能自行腐爛分解的肥皂,都會汙染水源。還有食物殘渣、魚類內臟
和骯髒的盤碟,都會造成污染。請協助維護用水系統的脆弱平衡,
請在距離湖泊或河川三十公尺以外,洗滌身體、衣服和盤碟,也請
不要在水中清洗魚類,最好是利用海水來作洗滌。請謹慎處理人類
的排泄物;請在距離營區和水源三十公尺以外,挖小洞,使用後掩
埋。請使用當地所提供的衛生設備,並將所有衛生紙和女性用品包
好帶走或燒燬。

Part

7

**160.** Which topic does the notice concern?
(A) Anti-contamination and eco-friendliness
(B) Protecting consumer rights
(C) Tour guide
(D) Rubbish dump

**161.** How may pets do fish any harm?
(A) Disordering their laying eggs
(B) Eating them up
(C) Keeping them on leash
(D) Biting them to death

**162.** What can be inferred from the passage?
(A) We can freely use sources of drinking water.
(B) Exploring a particular field is good for human beings.
(C) Toilet facilities are provided for hikers.
(D) Even decomposable products will be harmful to the environment.

中文翻譯

**160.** 本公告與何主題有關？　　　　　　　　解　答　**(A)**
(A) 反污染和善待自然
(B) 保護消費者的權益
(C) 旅遊指南
(D) 垃圾堆

**161.** 寵物對魚會造成什麼傷害？　　　　　　解　答　**(A)**
(A) 擾亂它們的產卵
(B) 把它們吃掉
(C) 把它們用皮帶繫住
(D) 把它們咬死

**162.** 從本文可以推論出什麼？　　　　　　　解　答　**(D)**
(A) 我們能夠自由利用飲水源。
(B) 探討特定的領域對人類有益。
(C) 衛生設備是提供給登山健行者 ( 遠足客 )。
(D) 即使能自行腐爛分解的產品也對環境有害。

---

註　解

- litter　　　v. 亂扔 ( 廢棄物 )
- pollute　　 v. 污染
- entrails　　n. 內臟 ( 尤指腸 )
- discreet　　a. 謹慎的
- waste　　　n. 廢棄物
- feminine　　a. 女性的
- rubbish dump 垃圾堆
- explore　　 v. 探討，勘查
- hiker　　　n. 登山健行者，遠足者

- biodegradable　　a. 能自行腐爛分解的
- scrap　　　　　　n. 殘渣，殘羹剩飯
- delicate　　　　 v. 脆弱的，細微的
- disposal　　　　 n. 丟棄處理
- facilities　　　　n. 設備
- anti-contamination n. 反污染
- infer　　　　　　v. 推論，斷定
- particular　　　　a. 特定的
- decomposable　　a. 可分解的

209　　　新 | 版 | 多 | 益 | 測 | 驗 | 攻 | 略

Part
7

Questions **163-165** refer to the following tip.

# *LEATHER CARE "DOs" and "DON'Ts"*

With proper care, your leather garments should last a very long time. Keep in mind that regular use enhances the appearance of your leather wear. So go ahead, wear your leather garments often.

## ● **Storage**

1. Keep in a well-ventilated, cool, dry place.
2. Store your leather wear on a well-shaped wooden, plastic or padded hanger.

## ● **Care**

1. Apply a high quality leather lotion on a soft cloth to clean and moisturize your finished leather. Hang dry.
2. If your leather becomes wet, allow it to dry naturally at room temperature. When dry, apply a leather protector.
3. Liquid stains should be gently cleaned with a damp cloth. If stains linger, clean with a leather cleaning solution.

## ● **"Don'ts"**

1. Don't put your leather wear in the dryer.
2. Don't store leather in direct sunlight or hot places such as attics or parked cars.
3. Don't use plastic bags for storing leather. This can cause excessive dryness.

中文翻譯

問題 163-165 請參考以下的建議。

# 皮件保養的 "正確" 與 "錯誤" 方法

適當的維護,你的皮衣應可保存非常持久。切記定期的穿用,會讓皮衣外觀更好看。所以,就請開始時多穿皮衣吧。

## ● 收藏

1. 保存在通風良好、涼爽、乾燥之處。
2. 將皮衣放置在外形良好的的木製、塑膠製或有墊料的衣架上。

## ● 維護

1. 用軟布沾高品質的皮革保養劑,來清潔並滋潤你的皮件。再掛起來晾乾。
2. 如果皮衣變潮,就讓它在室溫下自然風乾。風乾之後,使用皮革防護劑。
3. 液狀的污漬應用濕布輕輕擦拭。如果污漬難以清除,則使用皮革清潔劑。

## ● "不正確的方法"

1. 不要把皮衣放入烘乾機。
2. 不可把皮件直接存放在陽光下或酷熱處,例如頂樓或停放的車輛中。
3. 不可使用塑膠袋保存皮件。這會造成過度的乾燥。

Part

7

**163.** How should wet leather be treated?
(A) It should be hung outside.
(B) It should be dried in a dryer.
(C) It should be patted dry with a towel.
(D) It should be dried indoors.

**164.** When should a leather cleaning solution be used?
(A) Whenever a leather garment is stored
(B) When a dry cloth is ineffective
(C) When there is difficulty removing a stain
(D) Whenever a leather garment is stained

**165.** How can a leather garment's appearance be enhanced?
(A) By avoiding the use of hangers
(B) By wearing it frequently
(C) By storing it at room temperature
(D) By storing it in a plastic bag

中文翻譯

**163.** 受潮的皮件應該怎麼處理？ 　　解　答　**(D)**
(A) 應掛在室外。
(B) 應放進烘乾機烘乾。
(C) 應用毛巾拍打至乾。
(D) 應放在室內晾乾。

**164.** 何時應使用皮革清潔劑？ 　　解　答　**(C)**
(A) 收存皮衣時
(B) 乾布去漬無效時
(C) 污漬難以清除時
(D) 皮衣有污漬時

**165.** 皮衣的外觀如何能更好？ 　　解　答　**(B)**
(A) 避免使用吊衣架
(B) 常常穿它
(C) 收藏在室溫中
(D) 存放在塑膠袋內

註　解

| · proper | a. 恰當的，合適的 | · care | n. 照顧，保護 |
| · garment | n. 服裝，衣著 | · enhance | v. 提高價值 / 品質 |
| · well-ventilated | a. 通風良好的 | · lotion | n. 塗劑，清潔劑 |
| · moisturize | v. 增加水份，滋潤 | · protector | n. 保護物 |
| · damp | a. 潮濕的 | · stain | n. 污漬 |
| · linger | v. 長時間持續 | · solution | n. 溶液，溶劑 |
| · dryer | n. 烘乾機 | · attics | n. 閣樓，頂樓 |
| · plastic | a. 塑膠的 | · pat | v. 輕打，撫拍 |

Part
**7**

Questions **166-169** refer to the following e-mail.

| To: | bioservice@biochemhealth.com |
| From: | Valentina Erny < vaerny@twinpeaks.com > |
| Subject: | Return Shipment & Demand Reimbursement |
| Date: | May 21, 2010 |

Dear Sir / Ma'am,

I am writing this e-mail to you with regard to an order I placed 20 DAYS ago on May 1 via your on-line shopping Website. The order number was KM080401-678.

The order that I placed included the following products.
1. Titan Complex Vitamin, 3 bottles (100-pill size)
2. GraceEve Chlorella, 2 boxes (200-tablet size)
3. Hercules Herb Extract, 3 boxes (150-tablet size)

The total for the order was $195.95, including tax and priority shipping.

I received my order this morning 13 DAYS later than had been promised to me even though I paid an extra $8.00 for a holiday rush order. However, this was not the only problem. Upon opening the package, I noticed that there was only one box of chlorella tablets that I ordered two. The other one was not to be found anywhere. Furthermore, the cap on one of the Vitamin bottles had been completely torn off.

Because of this, I am returning the shipment to you. I hope that you will ship a new replacement order by express, as well as refund the cost of the priority shipping fee that I paid. I would also hope that you would reimburse the shipping fee for the return shipment that I am sending back to you. Please check your records, and send the replacement to me asap.

Thank you for your help,
Valentina Erny

中文翻譯

問題 170-172 請參考以下的建議。

旅館大廳的服務生，希望每件行李至少收小費 1 美元；在豪華的飯店，則是每件行李 2 美元，或數件行李 5 美元。不須給櫃檯人員、電梯操作員或是旅館服務台人員小費。但是，當抵達時，給看門的人員至少 1 美元是很平常的。如果他提供了特別的服務，則可以多給。給看門的人 1 元的小費，請他幫忙叫計程車是很標準的。每晚該付 2 美元給打掃旅館房間的女服務生，錢放在標明〝給女服務生〞的信封內。

**170.** Who is a tip UNnecessary for?
(A) The doorman
(B) The roommaid
(C) The desk clerk
(D) The bellboy

**171.** What is this passage about?
(A) A tip on tips
(B) A hotel ad.
(C) A want ad.
(D) A precaution

**172.** How much should you give the cleaner per night as a tip?
(A) $1
(B) $5
(C) $2
(D) $3

中文翻譯

**170.** 不需要給什麼人小費？　　　　　　　　解　答　**(C)**
(A) 看門的人員
(B) 房間女服務員
(C) 櫃台接待員
(D) 大廳服務生

**171.** 這篇文章是關於什麼？　　　　　　　　解　答　**(A)**
(A) 有關給小費的建議
(B) 旅館的廣告
(C) 求才廣告
(D) 預防措施

**172.** 你應該每晚給清潔工多少錢當作小費？　解　答　**(C)**
(A) 一美元
(B) 五美元
(C) 二美元
(D) 三美元

註　解

| | | | |
|---|---|---|---|
| · bellboy | n. 旅館大廳服務生 | · luxury | a. 豪華的，奢華的 |
| · desk clerk | 　櫃檯人員 | · concierge | n. 旅館服務台人員 |
| · doorman | 　看門的人 | · roommaid | n. 房間女服務生 |
| · envelope | n. 信封 | · precaution | n. 預防措施 |

Part

**7**

Questions **173-176** refer to the following directions.

# Phone Banking Directions

A Choose from the following options:

1. Bank Service Information
2. Balance / Transaction Inquiries
3. To report a lost or stolen card

4. Address / Account Changes
5. Current Exchange and Interest Rates
6. Customer Service

B Enter your 16-digit account number

C Enter your secret code

※ You can press "0" at any time to inquire with a Customer Service representative.

1. Account balances are of the current business day or as of the previous business day if calling between 4 p.m. and 9 a.m. weekdays.

2. Account balances are of the previous business day if calling on weekends and / or bank holidays.

3. Transactions done by phone after 4 p.m. will not be credited until the next business day.

4. Transactions such as inter-account transfers done by phone will not be credited until the next business day.

5. Address / Account changes done by phone are effective as of the following business day regardless of time.

中文 翻譯

問題 173-176 請參考以下的操作說明。

## 電 話 交 易 使 用 說 明

A 選擇下列選項：

1. 銀行服務資訊
2. 餘額 / 交易 查詢
3. 信用卡遺失或遭竊掛失
4. 地址 / 帳戶變更
5. 目前匯率和利率
6. 顧客服務

B 輸入您 16 位數的帳號

C 輸入您的密碼

※ 任何時候，您都可以按「0」洽詢客服人員。

1. 在週一至週五下午 4 點至上午 9 點之間來電查詢，帳戶餘額是當日或前一日的交易記錄。

2. 在週末或銀行假日來電查詢，帳戶餘額是前一日的交易記錄。

3. 下午 4 點以後經由電話的交易，於下一個營業日存入帳戶。

4. 經由電話轉帳的交易，於下一個營業日存入帳戶。

5. 經由電話變更地址、帳戶，無論何時，均須等到次一營業日始生效。

**173.** What kind of banking service is being offered?
(A) After service
(B) Audiovisual service
(C) Automated service
(D) Door-to-door service

**174.** When will an address change done on Friday at 2 p.m. be effective?
(A) Next Monday
(B) After 4 p.m.
(C) At the moment
(D) The current business day

**175.** When will a transaction done by phone at 5 p.m. be credited?
(A) On the current business day
(B) On the previous business day
(C) On the next business day
(D) On the bank holiday

**176.** What would you press for your account balance?
(A) 6
(B) 5
(C) 3
(D) 2

中文翻譯

**177.** 這趟旅遊將費時多久？
(A) 半個月
(B) 將近一星期
(C) 超過兩個月
(D) 兩三天

解　答　**(B)**

**178.** 遊客在這個地區要小心什麼？
(A) 野生動物
(B) 廢棄的水井
(C) 危險的水路
(D) 划獨木舟的人

解　答　**(C)**

**179.** 這個公園被描寫成什麼？
(A) 廢棄的地方
(B) 未開發的地區
(C) 花朵盛開的田野
(D) 崎嶇不毛之地

解　答　**(B)**

**180.** 這公園內的水路如何？
(A) 不安全的。
(B) 寧靜的。
(C) 崎嶇不平的。
(D) 暴風雨的。

解　答　**(A)**

註　解

- contemplate　v. 仔細考慮
- canoeist　n. 划獨木舟的人
- waterway　n. 水路，航道
- hardship　n. 困難，艱辛
- abandoned　a. 廢棄的
- flowery　a. 多花的
- tranquil　a. 平靜的，寧靜的
- circuit　n. 環行，環航
- wilderness　n. 蠻荒地區
- hazard　n. 危險
- stormbound　a. 被暴風雨困住的
- uncultivated　a. 未開墾的
- badlands　n. 荒原，不毛之地
- bumpy　a. 崎嶇的，不平的

Part 7

Questions **181-185** refer to the following e-mails.

| To: | Simon <simon@globalmate.com> |
|---|---|
| From: | Akio Nakamura <akionakamura@kchpr.com> |
| Subject: | How's it going? |

Simon,

How's it going? Haven't heard from you for quite some time.

I've been back in Tokyo for four months now. So far life's been fine to me. I am working for KCH Public Relations Company as a creative researcher. This company is quite young, but the officemates are really energetic. You've got to be here to feel their dynamic spirit. All people and things move around me at such a pace that it is never as dull as ditchwater. My job is quite heavy, but I must say I've learnt a lot from it and have made lots of good contacts.

I have to keep myself updated all the time, because living and working in Toyko is truly international. Toyko is a very cosmopolitan city and it's really a great place to train up newcomers.

Recently I got myself involved in a ninety-thousand-dollar project promoting a portfolio. Sure there were sleepless nights when planning for it. Yet I'm more excited and happier than I used to be. And how about you? How about your job?

Remember, all work and no play will make your life deadly boring!

Best Wishes,
Akio

中文 翻譯

問題 181-185 請參考以下的電子郵件。

| 收件者： | Simon <simon@globalmate.com> |
|---|---|
| 寄件者： | Akio Nakamura <akionakamura@kchpr.com> |
| 主旨： | 近來如何？ |

Simon,

　　近來如何？好長一段時間沒有你的消息了。

　　我已經回到東京四個月了。到目前為止，我的生活還不錯。我目前在 KCH 公關公司工作，當創意研究員。這家公司剛成立不久，但是同事們相當有活力。你應該到這兒來感受一下他們的朝氣。我周遭所有的人事物，行進步調從不令人乏味。我的工作非常繁重，但我必須說，我從中學到許多，同時也建立了不少良好的關係。

　　我必須讓自己隨時跟上時代腳步，因為在東京生活和工作，是非常國際性的。東京是一個相當世界性的都市，真的是訓練新手的好地方。

　　最近，我參與一件九萬美金的促銷投資組合方案。在策劃時，當然一連幾夜沒睡。但是我比以前更興奮、更快樂。你呢？你的工作怎樣呢？

　　切記，只是工作、沒有玩樂，會使生活非常無趣喔！

祝好！

Akio

| To: | Akio Nakamura <akionakamura@kchpr.com> |
| From: | Simon <simon@globalmate.com> |
| Subject: | About my job. |

Akio,

Thank you for your e-mail yesterday. It is true that I have not written to you for a couple of months. This e-mail should put you in the picture about my job.

As I said in the last e-mail, the launch of our automatic color press in China last fall was rather low-key. Competitors' machines are manufactured locally and marketed aggressively at irresistible prices. Up to now, imported machines like ours have been subject to 30% duty and 20% sales tax.

The only weakness of our machine has been its cost. The high price of the machine prohibits customers from buying it. And one of the main disadvantages for us has been our inability to find a highly motivated agent to promote our products. So we find it hard to gain market share here. Yet the intensively competitive pressure of the trade is favorable.

An article which appeared in last week's *Press Technology Weekly* praised the automatic color press highly. That sounds good for us. All for now. I hope you have a great success in your field.


Keep in touch.
Simon

| 收件者： | Akio Nakamura <akionakamura@kchpr.com> |
|---|---|
| 寄件者： | Simon <simon@globalmate.com> |
| 主旨： | 關於我的工作 |

Akio,

謝謝你昨天寄來的 e-mail。的確，我有幾個月沒寫信給你了。這封 e-mail 應該能讓你知道我的工作詳情。

就像我在上一封 e-mail 所說的，我們公司的自動彩色印刷機於去年秋天在中國上市，是相當低調的。競爭對手的機器在當地製造，同時以非常誘人的價錢積極推銷。直到現在，像我們進口的機器一直受限於 30% 的關稅和 20% 的營業稅。我們機器唯一的弱點，在於它的價格。機器的價錢高得讓顧客買不起。還有主要的不利因素之一，就是我們一直無法找到有意願的代理商，來推銷我們的產品。所以，我們發現在此地要佔有市場很困難。不過，業界激烈的競爭壓力總是好的。

在上星期的《印刷科技週刊》，登了一篇文章，對自動彩色印刷機給予極高得評價，對我們來說，那還真不錯。先談到這裡，我希望你在你那一行表現出色。

保持聯絡！

Simon

**181.** Which is NOT addressed in these e-mails?
(A) Trade pressure
(B) Printing press
(C) International city
(D) On-the-job training

**182.** What is Simon's e-mail mainly about?
(A) Overtime work
(B) Intense trade competition
(C) How to promote his company's products
(D) Promoting a portfolio

**183.** In Akio's e-mail, the idiom "dull as ditchwater" in paragraph 2, lines 5 and 6, is closest in meaning to _____.
(A) monotonous
(B) colourful
(C) adventurous
(D) censorious

中文翻譯

**181.** 兩篇 e-mail 中未提到什麼？ 　解　答　**(D)**
- (A) 同業壓力
- (B) 印刷機
- (C) 國際都市
- (D) 在職訓練

**182.** Simon 的 e-mail 主旨為何？ 　解　答　**(B)**
- (A) 加班工作
- (B) 激烈的同業競爭
- (C) 如何促銷他公司的產品
- (D) 促銷某種投資組合

**183.** 在 Akio 的 e-mail 中，第 2 段第 5、6 行的 　解　答　**(A)**
成語 "dull as ditchwater" 最接近哪個意思？
- (A) 單調的
- (B) 富有趣味的
- (C) 充滿新奇的
- (D) 吹毛求疵的

Part

**7**

**184.** How is the duty and tax of the imported press described?
(A) It is tax-deductible.
(B) It is tax-exempt.
(C) It is a heavy burden.
(D) It is duty-free.

**185.** According to the e-mail, which is the detriment to the imported color press?
(A) Irresistible price
(B) No aggressive agent
(C) Less advertising
(D) No customer service

---

**註　　解**

| | | | | | |
|---|---|---|---|---|---|
| · officemate | n. | 同事 | · energetic | a. | 有活力的，精神充沛的 |
| · dynamic | a. | 強而有力的，有活力的 | · pace | n. | 步調，步伐 |
| · (as) dull as ditchwater (dishwater) 非常乏味的 | | | | | |
| · contact | n. | 聯繫，社會關係 | · updated | a. | 最新的，不落伍的 |
| · cosmopolitan | a. | 世界性的 | · newcomer | n. | 新來者，新手 |
| · portfolio | n. | 投資組合 | · boring | a. | 乏味的，無聊的 |
| · put ... in the picture | 讓…知情 / 了解 | | · launch | n. | 發行，投入市場 |
| · press | n. | 印刷機；印刷 | · low-key | a. | 低調的 |
| · aggressively | adv. | 積極地 | | | |

中文翻譯

**184.** 進口印刷機的關稅和營業稅如何？　　　　　　解　答　**(C)**
(A) 可減免課稅的。
(B) 免稅的。
(C) 沉重的負擔。
(D) 免稅的。

**185.** 根據 e-mail 看來，對進口的彩色印刷機不　　解　答　**(B)**
利之處為何？
(A) 誘人的價格
(B) 沒有積極的代理商
(C) 少有廣告
(D) 無顧客服務

註　解

- irresistible　　a. 誘人的，不能抗拒的
- be subject to ...　受…約束 / 支配的，受制於…，取決於…
- duty　　　　　n. 關稅　　　　　　· prohibit　　　v. 禁止，防止
- disadvantage　n. 缺點，不利　　　· inability　　　n. 無能，沒辦法
- motivated　　a. 有積極性的　　　· competitive　a. 競爭的
- favorable　　n. 有利的，適宜的　· address　　　v. 對 ... 說話 / 演講
- overtime　　n. 加班；加班費　　· deductible　　a. 可減免 / 扣除的
- exempt　　　a. 被免除的　　　　· burden　　　n. 負擔，重擔
- detriment　　n. 不利，損害

Part
**7**

Questions **186-190** refer to the following reports.

Japanese adults by the hundreds of thousands — young and old — are going to classrooms across the islands to pursue new goals and fulfillment in life. Adults are now the fastest-growing segment of Japanese education and are likely to remain so for years to come. In 2009, about 5 million adult Japanese were attending school or college part time. Today the total comes to almost 9 million enrolled in instructional programs at college campuses, community centers, cram schools and medical centers. Classes adults are taking courses including sculpturing, painting, yoga relaxation, birdwatching, classical-music appreciation, photography, dancing and weaving. What educators are discovering is that many adults come back to school not just to fill time, or learn a job or hobby, but to enlarge their understanding of themselves, their lives and their relationship to the world around them.

中文翻譯

問題 186-190 請參考以下的報導。

**大**約有數十萬的日本成年人，不論老少，正在日本各島的課堂上，追求新的生活目標和滿足。成人現在是日本教育中成長最快速的部份，很可能在未來幾年也都依然如此。在 2009 年，大約有五百萬日本的成年人，利用部份時間進入學校或大學就讀。至今，總數將近九百萬人，參加了大學校園、社區中心、補習班和醫院所辦的教學課程。成人參加的課程包括雕塑、繪畫、瑜珈舒壓、賞鳥、古典音樂欣賞、攝影、舞蹈和編織。教育學者發現：許多成人回到學校，不只是為了消磨時間，或學習一項工作或嗜好，而是為了要擴增他們對自我、生活以及和周遭世界關係的瞭解。

Specialists find that 3 out of every 7 peole in our country are relaxing — away from paid jobs — in painting, performing music, weaving, wood carving and other hobbies. There are also estimates that about 10 percent of homes have ardent amateur gardeners who take care of greenery from house plants to large vegetable gardens. Two percent collect stamps and about 30 thousand are amateur photographers. An estimated 80 thousand regularly participate in organized dance courses.

One of the main reasons for the prosperity, observers say, is that our contemporary countrymen feel a deep need to escape the routine of their jobs. In leisure time, they turn to hobbies for a kind of individual self-expression and relaxation. For example, social psychologists say, most people choose hobbies in which at least a small amount of physical labor is involved. They also choose hobbies which provide immediate evidence of results. Such activities often are in contrast to their jobs, which involve many other people, no single one of whom can point to a product and say, "That was made entirely by me." Director Simon Liu of the Social Bureau says, "It's not just using your hands to make things. It's the sense of personal achievement that comes from doing a job from beginning to end."

專家發現：每七個國人當中，就有三個人放下謀生的工作，而悠遊於繪畫、音樂演奏、編織、木雕和其它嗜好。估計大約百分之十的家庭裡，有極為熱衷的業餘園丁，他們照料綠色植物，從室內盆栽到大的菜圃。有百分之二的國人會集郵，而大約有三萬人是業餘的攝影師。估計有八萬人定期參加舞蹈課程。

觀察家表示：這繁榮現象的主要原因之一，就是現代的國人深切覺得需要遠離他們每天一成不變的工作。閒暇時，他們轉向個人的嗜好，去尋求一種自我表現與舒解。社會心理學家表示：例如大多數人選擇的嗜好，是其中至少帶有些許體力活動的，他們也選擇能立刻展現成果的嗜好。這類的活動往往和他們的工作成對比。他們的工作涉及許多其他人，而沒有任何人能夠指著一項產品說：「它完全都是我做的。」社會局的劉主任表示：「那不只是用你的雙手去做出東西，那是從頭到尾把一件事情做好的個人成就感。」

**186.** What is implied in these reports?
(A) Hobbies are not participatory.
(B) Many adults have the urge to know and continue to grow.
(C) Many adults come back to school just for fun.
(D) Japanese want just to watch those talented artists.

**187.** According to these passages, which topic is appropriate?
(A) Learning has more meaning than it has purpose
(B) The warm feeling of achievement
(C) Self-renewal takes new directions in hobbies, back-to-school
(D) Hobbies are good for health

**188.** Which of the following is NOT discussed in these passages?
(A) Gardening
(B) Sculpturing
(C) Aerobics
(D) Antique collecting

**189.** What is the main explanation of why adults pick up new hobbies?
(A) Adults want to expand their interests.
(B) Hobbies have fulfilled adults' childhood dream.
(C) Adults intend to kill time.
(D) Hobbies often serve to focus self-awareness.

**190.** What is NOT mentioned as a reason for people choosing hobbies?
(A) People don't like unchangeable work.
(B) People like to relax themselves in leisure time.
(C) People often take part in activities which involve many other people.
(D) People don't like to make things entirely by themselves.

---

註　解

| | | | | | |
|---|---|---|---|---|---|
| • pursue | v. | 追求，追查 | • fulfillment | n. | 滿足；滿足感 |
| • segment | n. | 部份 | • instructional | a. | 指導的，教學用的 |
| • sculpture | v. | 雕刻 | • educator | n. | 教師，教育工作者 |
| • estimate | n. / v. | 估計；估算 | • greenery | n. | 綠色植物 |

中文翻譯

**186.** 從這些報導可得知什麼？　　　　　　　　解　答　**(B)**
　　(A) 業餘嗜好不是參與性的。
　　(B) 許多成年人有求知的衝動，且不斷成長。
　　(C) 許多成年人回到學校，純粹是為了好玩。
　　(D) 日本人只要看那些有天份的藝術家。

**187.** 根據這兩篇文章，哪個標題較適當？　　　　解　答　**(C)**
　　(A) 學習本身比其目的更有意義
　　(B) 溫暖的成就感
　　(C) 從嗜好、重回校園尋求自我改造新方向
　　(D) 嗜好對健康有益

**188.** 以下哪一項未在文中提及？　　　　　　　　解　答　**(D)**
　　(A) 園藝
　　(B) 雕刻
　　(C) 有氧舞蹈
　　(D) 收集古董

**189.** 成年人學習新嗜好的主因是什麼？　　　　　解　答　**(D)**
　　(A) 成年人要擴展興趣。
　　(B) 嗜好實現了孩提時代的夢想。
　　(C) 成年人打算消磨時間。
　　(D) 嗜好往往有助於自我覺醒。

**190.** 何者不是人們選擇業餘嗜好的理由？　　　　解　答　**(D)**
　　(A) 人們不喜歡一成不變的工作。
　　(B) 人們喜歡在閒暇時放鬆自己。
　　(C) 人們常參加涉及他人的活動。
　　(D) 人們不喜歡完全獨力完成東西。

註　解

| | | | |
|---|---|---|---|
| · regularly | adv. 定期地，經常 | · participate | v. 參加，參與 |
| · prosperity | n. 繁榮 | · observer | n. 觀察家 |
| · contemporary | a. 當代的 | · routine | n. 慣例，一成不變的事務 |
| · psychologist | n. 心理學家 | · labor | n. 工作（體力勞動） |
| · contrast | n. 與…相反 | · achievement | n. 成就，實現 |
| · aerobics | n. 有氧體操／運動 | · antique | n. 古董 |

Part
7

Questions **191-195** refer to the following advertisement and e-mail.

---

# *Help Wanted*

### People with Web page design abilities wanted!

If you already have a job but want to earn more money in your spare time, please tell us about your Web abilities. We are only interested in your ability to create the product. Now, let your creativity be a key to extra money!

If this appeals to you, please contact HR A.S.A.P. by email at webdesign@comsat.com

---

| To: | HR <webdesign@comsat.com> |
|---|---|
| From: | Marina Cott <marinac@duredu.com> |
| Subject: | Apply for a job |

To whom it may concern,

I'm writing to you in reference to the advertisement you have placed in the April 10th edition of the Financial Daily.

As you'll note in the enclosed résumé, I have had extensive experience in the field of computers. Since my graduation from UC Berkerly, I have had the chance to work with top firms in the computer industry. With my knowledge and expertise, I feel that I can be an asset to your company. I hope that you'll give me the opportunity to show this.

Please feel free to contact me at any time. I look forward to hearing from you.

Sincerely yours,

Marina Cott

# READIG COMPREHENSION

## 中文翻譯

問題 191-195 請參考以下的資訊。

---

### 徵 才 啟 事

**徵求有網頁設計才能的人！**

如果你已經有工作，而想利用空閒賺外快，請告訴我們你的網路專長。我們只在乎你創造商品的能力。現在就讓你的創意，賺取更多的錢！如果你對此有興趣，請儘快用 email 和人資部門聯絡，

email 信箱：webdesign@comsat.com

---

| 收件者： | 人力資源部 <webdesign@comsat.com> |
|---|---|
| 寄件者： | Marina Cott <marinac@duredu.com> |
| 主旨： | 應徵工作 |

敬啟者，

我看到 4 月 10 日金融日報你們所刊登的廣告，因此來信應徵。

在附件的履歷表上您會看到，我在電腦方面有非常豐富的經驗。我從 Berkerly 大學畢業以後，就有機會在電腦業的好幾家頂尖的公司工作。以我的知識和專業技能，我認為我會成為貴公司的資產。希望您給我機會證明。

請隨時和我聯絡，期待收到您的回音。

Marina Cott
敬上

**191.** What kind of the email is it?
(A) A cover letter
(B) An e-mail to the columnist
(C) An e-mail of recommendation
(D) A résumé

**192.** What kind of person could not do this job?
(A) A person who only has weekends off
(B) A person with no free time
(C) An engineer
(D) A college student

**193.** Why was this e-mail written?
(A) To reply to an ad
(B) To apply for a job
(C) To keep in touch with someone
(D) To sell computers

**194.** Which characteristic would be best for this job?
(A) Sense of humor
(B) Diligence
(C) Loyalty
(D) Inventiveness

**195.** Which of the following is essential to this job?
(A) Ability to create Web pages
(B) Experience at a Web company
(C) New approach to management
(D) Working hours

註　解

| | | | |
|---|---|---|---|
| · spare | a. 多餘的，空閒的 | · creativity | n. 創造力 |
| · appeal | v. 吸引，引起興趣 | · contact | v. 與…聯繫 |
| · in reference to ... 關於… | | · edition | n. 一期或一版 |
| · note | v. 注意 | · enclosed | a. 附加的，附寄的 |
| · résumé | n. 履歷，簡歷 | · extensive | a. 廣博的，大量的 |

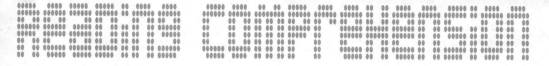

中文翻譯

**191.** 這是何種 e-mail？　　　　　　　　　解答 **(A)**
(A) 一封附函
(B) 給專欄作家的 e-mail
(C) 一封推薦 e-mail
(D) 一份履歷表

**192.** 哪種人不能從事這項工作？　　　　　解答 **(B)**
(A) 只有週末有空的人
(B) 沒有空閒的人
(C) 工程師
(D) 大專生

**193.** 為何寫這封 e-mail？
(A) 回覆廣告　　　　　　　　　　　　解答 **(B)**
(B) 應徵工作
(C) 和某人聯絡
(D) 銷售電腦

**194.** 什麼特質最適合這項工作？
(A) 幽默感　　　　　　　　　　　　　解答 **(D)**
(B) 勤奮
(C) 忠誠
(D) 有創造力

**195.** 下列何者是這項工作的必備條件？
(A) 製作網頁的能力　　　　　　　　　解答 **(A)**
(B) 有網路公司的經驗
(C) 新的管理方法
(D) 工作時間

註　解

| | | | |
|---|---|---|---|
| · field | n. 領域，範圍 | · expertise | n. 專業技能 / 知識 |
| · asset | n. 資產，財產 | · cover letter | 附函 |
| · columnist | n. 專欄作家 | · recommendation | a. 推薦，介紹 |
| · characteristic | n. 特點，特性，特色 | · diligence | n. 勤奮 |
| · essential | a. 絕對必要的 | · approach | n. 方法，方式 |

Part
**7**

## Questions **196-200** refer to the following letter and order form.

### ▤ Financialweekly

Date: March 31, 2010

Dear Past Subscriber,

As our valued reader, we are happy to bring you an exceptional offer from Financialweekly. We are offering an exclusive and irresistible rate to past readers!

The global finance is reeling under rapid change in economic situations of most areas. Keeping up with financial events is difficult enough, not to mention understanding their full effects and how they will unfold. Financialweekly can help you understand!

With Financialweekly you'll get the key whys and wherefores on every report and you'll be among the first to know about significant financial events, ahead of any mass media.

You can have the benefit of this very special renewal subscription offer and have Financialweekly delivered to your home or office, at a privileged price of up to 60% less than what you would pay at the newsstand or bookstore.

We urge you to send back the order form below today and join the worldwide team of well-informed Financialweekly readers again. You'll appreciate Financialweekly's professional and forward-looking perspective at the beginning of the 21st century.

Yours sincerely,

*Thomas Guoa*

Thomas Guoa
General Manager
Asia Edition

P.S. # If you're ever dissatisfied, for any reason, you may cancel your subscription and receive a full refund on all unmailed issues. No questions asked.

A 'Best Buy' 78-issue subscription saves you NT$7,488 and at 52-issue subscription saves you NT$4,576. Please remember to return your order form before July 31, 2010.

Financialweekly's cover price is NT$160. For enquiries, please call (8862)2389-9808, fax (8862)2389-9167 or email us at: best.service@financialweekly.com.tw

中文翻譯　問題 196-200 請參考以下的信件和訂閱單。

---

### ≣≣≣ 金 融 週 刊

日期：2010 年 3 月 31 日

親愛的老訂戶，

　　您是我們重視的讀者，《金融週刊》很樂意為您帶來一份特別好禮。我們要提供給老訂戶一個獨享的、非常誘人的價錢！

　　在大部份地區經濟情況快速改變之下，全球金融正迅速衰退。要隨時了解金融狀況已經不容易，更不用說明白它們全面性的影響，以及它們將如何發展。《金融週刊》能夠幫助您了解狀況！

　　藉由《金融週刊》的每篇報導，您將得知關鍵原因，同時您將比大眾媒體優先得知重要的金融活動。

　　您可以得到這個特別的續訂戶優惠好禮，讓《金融週刊》繼續送到您府上或辦公室，比您在書報攤或書店購買，最高可省 **60%** 的價錢。

　　建議您今天就把下面的訂單寄回，再度加入全世界消息靈通的《金融週刊》讀者的行列。您將在 21 世紀的開始，充分了解《金融週刊》具專業和前瞻性的觀點。

亞洲版 總經理

*Thomas Guoa*

Thomas Guoa
敬上

附註：# 無論任何理由，不問原因，只要您不滿意，可以取消訂閱，並取回未滿期數的全額退款。「最優惠」訂閱 78 期可省下新台幣 7,488 元，而訂閱 52 期可省下新台幣 4,576 元。請記得在 2010 年 7 月 31 日之前，寄回您的訂閱單。

金融週刊每本定價新台幣 160 元。如有疑問，請洽詢 (8862)2389-9808，傳真 (8862)2389-9167 或 e-mail：best.service@financialweekly.com.tw

Part

**7**

# Financialweekly Special Subscription Order Form

**SAVE UP TO 60%**

Special subscription offer for Past Subscriber

Please tick:

- ☑ 18 months ( 78 issues ) at NT$ 64 per copy for a tatal of NT$4,922
- ☐ 12 months ( 52 issues ) at NT$ 72 per copy for a tatal of NT$3,744

Valid until: July 31, 2010  (DM0708TW)

*PAYMENT METHOD:*

- ☐ Bill me later
- ☑ Please charge to Credit Card
  ( Indicate which )

  | ☐ Visa | ☑ MasterCard | **Card Expiry Date** Month / Year |
  | ☐ JCBCard | ☐ Amex | 03   2013 |

**Card Number**

5468-4700-0262-8400

**Your Signature**

Amy Kao

**Telephone No.**

(8862)23899145

**E-mail Address**

amykao@toeicmate.com.tw

45433727          DM0708TW

**MS  AMY KAO**

**P O  BOX 33-200 TAIPEI**
**TAIPEI CITY 10099, TAIWAN, ROC**

Once subcribed, you may be contacted for the purposes of market reserch and / or direct marketing. Please tick here if you prefer not to be contacted for these purposes by:

- ☑ Financialweekly International
- ☑ Other companies

## MONEY BACK GUARANTEE

If you're ever  dissatisified, for any reason, you may cancel your subscription and receive a full refund on unmailed issues. No questions asked.

# 金 融 週 刊 特 別 訂 購 單

給 老 訂 戶 的 特 別 訂 閱 優 惠 好 禮

最高節省 **60%**

請勾選：

- ☑ 18 個月（78 期）每期新台幣 **64** 元，總共 **4,922** 元。
- ☐ 12 個月（52 期）每期新台幣 **72** 元，總共 **3,744** 元。

有效期限至 2010 年 7 月 31 日止 (DM0708TW)

付費方式：

- ☐ 寄帳單給我
- ☑ 信用卡付款
  (請註明)

☐ Visa  ☑ MasterCard  ☐ JCBCard  ☐ Amex

信用卡有效期限
月 / 年
03    2013

信用卡卡號
5468-4700-0262-8400

您的簽名
Amy Kao

電話 .
(8862)23899145

電子郵件信箱
amykao@toeicmate.com.tw

45433727                    DM0708TW

**中華民國台灣台北市 10099**
**台北郵政第 33-200 號信箱**

**高艾米　小姐**

訂閱後，您可能會收到市場調查或直銷聯絡電話。如果您不願受訪，請在此打勾：

- ☑ 國際金融週刊
- ☑ 其他公司

## 退 款 保 證

無論任何理由，不問原因，只要您不滿意，可以取消訂閱，並取回未滿期數的全額退款。

Part **7**

**196.** What is the purpose of the letter？
(A) To do a market research
(B) To push a marketing campaign
(C) To contact the reader to renew his subscription
(D) To offer the reader a special gift

**197.** By what date should renewal subscribers respond to Financialweekly？
(A) March 31
(B) July 31
(C) payday
(D) anytime

**198.** What did Thomas Guoa send with his letter?
(A) Subscription order form
(B) Price list
(C) "Best Buy" offer
(D) Full refund

**199.** How much can you save when you place a one-year subscription order?
(A) NT$4,922
(B) NT$3,744
(C) NT$4,576
(D) NT$7,488

**200.** In the letter, the phrase "whys and wherefores" in paragraph 3, line 1, is closest in meaning to _____.
(A) the reasons and explanations
(B) cause and effect
(C) research and development
(D) perfection and defect

註　解

| | | | |
|---|---|---|---|
| · exclusive | a. 獨有的，獨享的 | · irresistible | a. 不可抗拒的，誘人的 |
| · reel | v. 迅速後退 | · keep up with | 不斷了解；跟上 |
| · effect | n. 影響 | · unfold | v. 發展，展開 |
| · whys and wherefores 原因，理由 | | · significant | a. 重要的 |

中文翻譯

**196.** 這封信的目的是什麼？　　　　　　　　　解　答 **(C)**
(A) 作市場調查
(B) 推廣行銷活動
(C) 聯繫讀者續訂雜誌
(D) 給讀者特別好禮

**197.** 續訂戶在哪一天之前，要回覆金融週刊？　解　答 **(B)**
(A) 3 月 31 日
(B) 7 月 31 日
(C) 發薪日
(D) 任何時候

**198.** Thomas Guoa 隨信附寄什麼？　　　　　　解　答 **(A)**
(A) 訂閱單
(B) 價目表
(C) " 最優惠 " 好禮
(D) 全額退款

**199.** 訂閱一年期可以省多少？　　　　　　　　解　答 **(C)**
(A) 新台幣 4,922 元
(B) 新台幣 3,744 元
(C) 新台幣 4,576 元
(D) 新台幣 7,488 元

**200.** 信中第 3 段第 1 行的片語 "whys and　　　解　答 **(A)**
wherefores" 最接近哪個意思？
(A) 理由，原因
(B) 因果關係
(C) 研究發展
(D) 完美與缺陷

註　解

| | | | |
|---|---|---|---|
| · mass media | 大眾傳媒 | · renewal | n. 續期，待續 |
| · subscription | n. 訂閱 | · privileged | a. 享有特權的 |
| · well-informed | a. 消息靈通的 | · foward-looking | a. 前瞻性的 |
| · perspective | n. 觀點 | · dissatisfied | a. 不滿意的 |
| · refund | n. 退款 | · enquiry | n. 詢問 |

Part

**7**

國家圖書館出版品預行編目資料

新版多益測驗攻略 ＝ New TOEIC Preparation Guide II,
200 TOEIC test questions. --修訂再版. -- 臺北市：全球
模考, 民99. 06
　　面；　　公分

ISBN 978-986-6515-10-1（平裝附光碟片）

1. 多益測驗　2. 試題　3. 考試指南

805. 1895　　　　　　　　　　　　　　97014860

# 新版多益測驗攻略
# New TOEIC
# Test-Preparation Guide 2

| | | |
|---|---|---|
| 作　　　　者 | / | 高志豪・羽角俊之 |
| 發　行　人 | / | 高志豪 |
| 特　別　助　理 | / | 周嘉蕙 |
| 教　學　總　監 | / | 李淑娟 |
| 編　　　譯 | / | 楊素慧 |
| 資　訊　總　監 | / | 劉聖仕 |
| 美　術　編　輯 | / | 劉欣茹 |
| 出　版　者 | / | 全球模考股份有限公司 |
| 地　　　址 | / | 台北市忠孝西路一段41號5樓之5 |
| 全球模考官網 | / | www.globalmate.com.tw |
| 全球線上模考中心 | / | online.globalmate.com.tw |
| 電　　　話 | / | (02)2389-9808 |
| 傳　　　真 | / | (02)2389-9167 |

| | | |
|---|---|---|
| 印　　　刷 | / | 年代印刷企業有限公司 |
| 地　　　址 | / | 台北縣中和市建一路175號8樓 |
| 電　　　話 | / | (02)8221-4216 |
| 傳　　　真 | / | (02)8221-5213 |

出版日期 / 中華民國九十九年六月四日 修訂再版一刷

1書1CD・定價 / 新台幣 **350** 元・特價 / 新台幣 **300** 元